I0835972

UNEQUAL LOVES

Gazebo Books
PO Box 375
Summer Hill
New South Wales 2130
Australia
gazebobooks.com.au

First published 2025

An earlier version of 'The New Capital' was published in Griffith Review, No. 34: 'The Annual Fiction Edition' (October 2011).

National Library of Australia
Cataloguing-in-Publication Entry
Author: Xavier Hennekinne
Unequal Loves
First edition
ISBN 9781763600959

Cover and interior design by Mountains Brown Press
Cover and frontispiece art by Phil Day, photographed by Matt Stanton

UNEQUAL LOVES

xavier hennekinne

GAZEBO BOOKS SUMMER HILL 2025

Contents

The New Capital

The following year they went to Japan.

They landed at Kansai Airport at night and caught a train to Shin-Osaka. In the morning, after an early breakfast, they took the fast train to Okayama and then changed for an omnibus to Matsuyama. In Matsuyama, in front of the station, they took a taxi to the hotel where she had booked a Western-style room. They thought of walking, but it was raining lightly, and they agreed that it was not worth hauling their big suitcase in the rain, even though the hotel did not seem far according to the map. The hotel was not far from the station, though a little further than he had anticipated, and the cab fare came to almost a thousand yen. During the ride he glanced at the map of the city and recognised the park where the Ehime Museum of Art nestled. He pointed out the upper roof of the Matsuyama-jō castle to his wife. The castle was barely visible in the trees and mist on top of the hill, behind the park. They turned off into another avenue and left the park and castle behind. Halfway up the avenue, a few hundred metres past the park, the taxi rolled to a stop and the back doors automatically opened. When they got out of the car, the driver had unloaded their backpack and big suitcase onto the pavement in front of the hotel.

Their room was very, very small. They could not find a spot to open their suitcase. The room had a double bed with bedside tables, a desk, a tall, narrow wardrobe, and a large black massage chair, like those they had seen in airports in Asia, but without a coin slot. The chair had a control panel in the right armrest. He was not likely to sit in it.

He lifted the suitcase onto the bed and they emptied its contents into the wardrobe and onto the bathroom's faux-marble bench. What they did not put away in the wardrobe or bathroom they put on the desk: books he had brought with him and the recent issues of *The New Yorker* magazine he had not had the time to read when, in the evenings, he had researched their Japan holiday plans.

He had decided to read *The Old Capital* by Yasunari Kawabata during the trip. He had started the novel at home, just before leaving. This was perfect – they would spend a few days in Kyoto, where the story takes place, and in Tokyo they would stay in the district of Asakusa, where Kawabata lived in the 1920s and early 1930s.

His wife had said that he was taking too many books: he would not read them all. He had responded that he read a lot on holidays. 'Not that much,' she had said.

From the small window, which they could not open, they looked out onto the leafy side of a hill. It was good to be on holidays. It was good to be in Japan. Even if it rained lightly.

He was very excited; holidays, somehow, always started as a promise. A promise of change. The holiday in Japan built up such excitement in him that one would think he had been offered a new and wonderful life. He could become Japanese, settle down somewhere in Shikoku, and not go back to the office. Only after a few days would he emerge from the delusion and once more come to terms with the reality that holidays were not going to permit him to start again, with a clean slate.

Although he had always been interested in Japan, he had never visited it until now. In his early twenties he would say that he was passionate about Japan. His aunt Edmonde knew Japanese literature and had advised him to read writers of the Meiji and Taishō periods. So he read a few novels, mostly by Mori Ōgai and Shiga Naoya. He also watched several movies when they came out at the art-house cinemas of the fifth *arrondissement* (one of them was *In the Realm of the Senses*). These books and movies had impressed him. At the time he thought a lot about them. He had thought that if he were one day to write a novel he would write it like a Japanese novelist. His sentences would be delicate and graceful, like the steps of a cat.

When he moved to Sydney, he kept reading the classic novels, now in their English translations. But he had not done what one of his favourite authors, Nicolas Bouvier, had done: pack his bag and travel through Japan for many months. Only now, with his wife, was he going to travel through Japan, for two weeks, starting in Matsuyama.

In the light rain, under the transparent, bell-shaped umbrellas they had borrowed at the hotel, they walked down the avenue to the Ehime Museum of Art. When the concierge had handed them the umbrellas, he had remarked to his wife, 'Look, these umbrellas are see-through!' He was certain that, like him, she had never used a transparent umbrella before, but the smile she flashed at him told him she was not surprised by the object's design. On the map the museum was opposite the Athletic Ground, but today the Athletic Ground was a flat, muddy construction site with bulldozers coming and going seemingly without purpose.

They locked their umbrellas in the umbrella lockers and bought a ticket to all the current exhibitions, permanent and temporary.

The works in the main temporary exhibition were by Seison Maeda – paintings on silk, canvas, wood, and paper; a few ink drawings accompanied them. They depicted dogs, ducks, cormorants, grey mullet, peonies in a blue round vase, peach blossoms in a white-and-red vase, a young or old man or woman in a kimono (holding a musical instrument, kneeling before a bottle of sake or a jewellery box), naked women bathing, women elegantly dressed visiting an exhibition and holding their thin rectangular purses in front of their stomach or under their right arm, village scenes with minuscule people, forests, mountains, a bridge, a temple, and of Seison himself.

What he saw that day, he had never seen before in any of the museums and art galleries he had visited. The silk paintings stirred him. To his eyes the paintings had a radiant quality, a clarity and a shine. He imagined he was looking at them through a pair of miraculous glasses that had cured myopia or cataracts, revealing to those who had apparently perfect vision that they had not in fact had perfect vision until now. The silk seemed to capture the ambient light, depriving its surroundings of it, and to consume the pigments of the colours while intensifying them, like a star consuming and producing energy at the same time.

Such was his excitement that he had walked briskly, almost hurrying from one picture to the next. He was now at the end of the exhibition, at the entrance to the souvenir shop. He retraced his steps to the room where his wife was standing in front of a watercolour, reading the sign affixed to its lower right-hand corner. The painting was of a white cat on a yellow carpet.

'You're fast!' she said. 'Will you remember any of these paintings?'

The truth was that he probably would not, not in detail. Now that the light filtering into the rooms through the roof windows had turned into a warm, enveloping spring glow, he was drawn to look again at the paintings he had seen earlier in the wan light. He told his wife he wished to look again at the Maeda pictures. She exclaimed without articulating a word.

'I'll meet you at the souvenir shop,' he said.

After the museum they took an old German tram to Dōgo Onsen, the famous public baths. There they were offered three options: a bath; a bath and tea in the common tearoom; and a bath and tea in a private tearoom. They chose the third option, but no private room was available for tea after bathing, so they settled for option two, taking tea in the common room.

This was his first time in a public bath. By the large, steaming bath he washed quickly at one of the showers, sitting on a low wooden stool so his legs folded, as if squatting rather than sitting.

The water in the stone bath was much hotter than he would have it at home. He entered the water slowly and sat like the other naked men, facing the large copper tap from which water ran incessantly.

All the men looked straight ahead, at the tap and the marble wall. No one talked. He looked at the other bathers. Most were Japanese; only he and another were Caucasian. No one seemed to look at the others, so he too started to stare at the faucet. Men came and went. All, whether they were coming or going, had showers. It seemed you had to shower before entering the bath and again on leaving it. Most men did not stay long in the bath. By the time he decided to leave to join his wife in the tearoom, many men had come and gone.

When he returned to the common tearoom, dressed in one of the *onsen*'s yukata, his wife was talking with a Western couple, and he took the stairs up to the private tearooms.

Up the stairs, at the end of the third-floor corridor, a sliding door was open. He walked down and entered the small, quiet corner room.

The room had windows the whole length of two

perpendicular walls, which to him felt unusual. It looked out onto a narrow lane on one side and over the square on the other, where the old wooden façade of the onsen could be admired

Once again he became aware of the spring afternoon light, which brought warmth to the room. The fading light projected luminous geometric shapes onto the walls, their angles growing sharper as he stood peacefully, looking around the room.

On the walls, black and white photographs showed the same elegantly dressed man, alone or in a crowd, or sitting in a rickshaw.

An old woman in the onsen staff's kimono came into the room and surprised him, but before she could order him to go back downstairs, he asked her in English who the gentleman in the photos was. It was Sōseki Natsume, she said, who had often come to the baths and had had tea in the very room where they were standing. She explained that Sōseki

Natsume's fondness for baths had been given to a foolish character named Botchan in his novel of the same name. She then ordered him to return to the common tearoom at once. Which he did.

The Western couple had gone, and his wife, sitting in the same position on the *tatami*, was sipping tea, looking out onto the street.

'Where were you?' she asked when he knelt next to her.

'In Sōseki's room. Upstairs,' he said.

He picked up a small cup and poured tea from the teapot into it. He recognised the strong fragrance of smoked tea. They drank in silence. He thought of Sōseki's room and remembered the young Botchan from the book he had read a long time ago. His wife looked out onto the sloping, leafy street.

§

In Kyoto, they began with the art museums.

They rode the bicycles they had rented at the *ryokan* to the National Museum of Modern Art.

Again, in the museum, he was ahead of his wife. He moved from room to room hastily until he found himself before a painting by Tatsu Hirota titled *In a Pensive Mood.*

The young woman in a pensive mood was not particularly pretty. Her short hair seemed thin; her face was very round, with a small nose and mouth and long, narrow eyes. But she had youth.

She was undressing, it occurred to him. Her red *obi* was tangled in her black kimono, which was patterned with full, purple iris flowers. She held her kimono before her pubis and legs in a poised gesture. Her disrobing was suspended so she could admire her breasts, as large and round as her face, he thought, and perhaps avoid looking at the lower part of her body. Yes, she was looking at herself in a mirror – unseen by the viewer – admiring what she regarded as the most aesthetically pleasing part of her body. The old painter had painted a young woman, inspired, excited by her youthful breasts.

He could not take his eyes off her breasts. He remained standing before the picture, as if assured that no other work in the museum could tell him anything he did not already know, as if it had fully satisfied some curiosity…

He had never been sexually aroused by a work of art, at least not that he could recall. This picture captivated him, and he looked at it shamelessly. His mind started to elaborate a single, simple erotic scenario based on her breasts and her bottom, which he imagined to be plump.

On the way out they stopped at the museum's souvenir shop, where he bought a postcard of the painting and a book of pictures of selected paintings from the museum, which included *In a Pensive Mood*.

Later, back in their room, when looking closely at the painting and the two-line biography of the painter in the book, he saw that, yes, the artist had been old – eighty-four – when *In a Pensive Mood* was painted. Yet he was astonished to discover that the old painter was a woman.

§

The wave of tourists at Kinkaku-ji almost carried them through the temple grounds. They could only move their legs and move forward. He kept his right hand on their camera. He looked up when the crowd stopped and he and his wife were no longer moving forward. By standing on tiptoe and craning his neck to see beyond the tourists, he glimpsed a pond and, beyond it, a pavilion floating on the water, covered in gold.

For some reason he had forgotten that the Golden Temple was in Kyoto; he had not thought about it when he and his wife decided on the itinerary. They had merely listed names of the main Kyoto temples from the guidebooks without reading the paragraph on each temple. His mind had made no connection between these names and the Golden Temple. So it was a shock to be standing there in front of the pavilion of Mishima's novel.

A friend, he remembered, *his* friend, had given him a new French translation of *The Temple of the Golden Pavilion* for his nineteenth birthday. He and his friend lived in different cities and wrote to each other several times a week. She had written a note in the book, and for many nights after it arrived in the letterbox he could not sleep until the early hours, wondering whether he should respond to the note with a frank admission of his feelings for her or send her a book he admired in return, to thank her.

In the note she had called him her 'incestuous brother'.

What does 'incestuous brother' mean in relation to us, he kept asking himself during those sleepless nights. Does it mean that to her I am a brother and should not contemplate physical engagement with her? Am I incestuous because I desire her sexually? But how does she know for sure I desire her? I guess she knows, he thought, though he desired her some days and others not. Or are they both being incestuous in their intermittent desire? And wouldn't it be wise not to be incestuous to preserve the bond that normally joins sister and brother?

But now, at the temple, with the anguish of these sleepless nights over thirty years ago coming back to him, it occurred to him that perhaps she had meant for them to *become* incestuous. It was their fate, perhaps, for them to be as close as brother and sister could be, and to sleep together.

Had they not been *incestuous* in Carcassonne a year or two before she sent the book? he suddenly thought. During these sleepless nights, and until now, he had overlooked what had happened during the few days they had spent together in Carcassonne. These few days had been ranged away in a short story he wrote when he was eighteen and only now it occurred to him that it must have been then and there that she had conceived the idea of him as her incestuous brother.

He had thanked her for the book in his next letter. At that time, he had no money to buy a book for her and post it. He had not brought up the note in his letter.

After Carcassonne, they had not become lovers. Nor had they been before. Not in the strict sense. They were never in the mood at the same time.

They had kissed in the rain once in the summer. A

fair had been set up in the town's square for a week. A storm surprised them on their walk back from the fair to her mother's house. Against a tree they kissed in the warm rain, and then, still all wet, under a bus shelter. They had kissed and licked the warm rain off each other's faces. The warm rain, he had thought later, had done something to them. When they were back at her mother's place his timidity, the fear caused by his sexual inexperience got the better of him and he went straight to bed, alone. He remembered that his friend was disappointed but seemed to understand why he had then avoided her. After that summer, when they were sixteen, they wrote to each other frequently and visited each other about once a year.

They learned about each other and each other's lives in the letters. Sometimes they sent tapes with music they wanted the other to hear, and when they had earned a little money from their holiday jobs, they sent paperbacks.

They both frequented libraries. In their letters they often said: I have read such and such book, and I wish I could send it to you. They often wrote about the books they had read.

They were attentive to what the other said and meant. They made great efforts to write in such a way that the other would reveal something of herself or himself in the next letter. I wonder what you would make of this, one would write about an event or something seen in the street. Tell me something, tell me when you've read it, what the book did to you, the other would demand. Such a letter had accompanied the new translation of *The Temple of the Golden Pavilion*. The letter did not say: Tell me what you make of the note I wrote in the book.

His wife took several photos of the pavilion and of him in front of it. He took a photo of his wife in front of the pavilion. The photo showed the pond and on it the pavilion, as if the three-storey building were made of paper and could float, and it showed his wife's bust. They asked another tourist to take a photo of both of them in front of the pavilion.

Then they walked up the hill, behind the temple. He kept turning back to look at the brilliant edifice. Would he ever see it again?

They reached another smaller pond where, on a small island, stood a small stone tower that resembled a pagoda in the way it had several levels, like miniature storeys, and at each level, a sculpted skirt roof. It was hard to judge the tower's height from that distance, but it could not have been taller than he was. It was on that path, by the pond with the stone tower, that the narrator of the novel meets his friend Tsurukawa. It was clear that this is where the scene occurred. He told his wife, who, half interested, said, 'Yes?'

She had not read the novel. 'It's a great novel,' he said, and told her the story culminating in the burning of the temple – on the very grounds of which they stood. 'It is a novel about beauty.'

Upon saying these words he stopped walking. He looked around, dazed, gripped by a sudden thought: 'When did I cease preoccupying myself with beautiful things? Why have I neglected for so long finding, seeking rather, beauty?' Now, here, beauty was everywhere he turned; every single thing – the old gates of the temples, the blossoms of the cherry tree, but also of the magnolia and lime trees, the meticulousness in the arrangement of the rock gardens, the simplicity of the tea utensils, the light and colours in silk paintings, the memory of his friend... every single thing here, whether it belonged to the realm of the artificial, natural or cognitive, moved him. Every single thing also pointed to the shameful condition he found himself in: for many years now, he had been impervious to beauty.

His wife was walking up the path trodden by

the multitude of tourists. He started walking again, slowly, as if what had stopped him in his tracks had been a stitch in his side. He thought he needed to clear his mind – but his mind was already clear. He increased the speed and length of his stride. He focused on his wife's back, on catching up with his wife. By the time he reached her he could walk at a good pace again.

He and his friend had often talked about beauty. Of the essence of things. She would write about her lovers, how old or young they were, and how, whether they were university professors or delivery men from a furniture shop, they made her curious and offered stimulating conversations. Most were good lovers. But none of them knew her. No one, not even the university professor with whom the affair lasted over a year, could possibly know her, save for her friend – him – him and her mother. She would write about her mother. About how her father had aimed a rifle at her once and they had had to move far away from him. About how her mother taught French in a small suburban school and how teaching French had to be the most meaningful profession one can spend one's life doing…

The young acolyte in Mishima's book thought the shadow of the temple more beautiful than the temple itself. The memory of his and his friend's feelings toward each other was more beautiful than the feelings themselves, though until now, the beauty in the memory of the feelings or the feelings themselves had not been evident. He was not nostalgic; until now, he had seen these feelings as a puzzle he had abandoned long ago.

These feelings, today, were beautiful not because they contained love or passion or were complex and changed shape like shadows, but because they had been temporary, to be lost, left to memories.

He remembered how he had written to his friend

about small things he saw now and then, in the streets or elsewhere, on his way somewhere. Things that would only last a moment, then disappear, in pure loss. 'Pure loss' was what he then called the transient, where he saw beauty. Not realising that their relationship too had been transient, in the end, pure loss, and that its beauty would reveal itself over thirty years later in Kyoto.

Beauty had somehow abandoned his everyday life. Back home, beauty would disappear again, or perhaps what was not in front of him, what was not immediate, was going to be beautiful: Japan, the gardens and the temples, the memory of the kiss in the rain, the many letters received and written, receiving the book, and reading the note inscribed inside, being 'the incestuous brother'.

He could not tell his wife. He would not know where to start. It was too complicated. He felt lazy and felt that he was not good at speaking about his feelings, especially to his wife. At dinner, in a small restaurant where they were sitting on the floor, he said, 'Kyoto is beautiful, isn't it?'

She smiled. 'Yes.'

On the white wall in the box where they sat, behind his wife a scene depicting geishas skiing had been painted in great detail and the light of a projector framed the painting in a bluish circle.

They managed to order a beef dish – '*gyoniku*' he had said to the waitress – and dishes he randomly pointed to in the menu. And some tea and cold sake.

'We should travel more,' his wife said. She meant travelling abroad.

He agreed. Perhaps it would be good for him to travel abroad without his wife, alone. But the days when he could do such things were long gone, he thought.

The dishes arrived one by one. Despite not

knowing what they had ordered, they had chosen well. The beef slices were thin and fine and melted in their mouths.

The young acolyte in Mishima's book burns the temple down because he cannot suffer the beauty of its timelessness.

His friend broke off their friendship when he had invited her, during one of her visits to Paris, to stay with him and the young woman he was now living with. He had also told his friend that he was considering proposing to the young woman.

His friend had made the trip, but when he picked her up at the train station, she refused to go to the apartment he was sharing with the young woman.

'Where do you want to go, then?' he asked.

'I don't know, but not to her place,' she answered.

'What do you mean, *not to her place*? It is also my place and there is nowhere else to go.'

'I'll stay at a hotel.'

She checked into a cheap hotel on the other side of town. It was not going to be convenient for them to meet, and it had irritated him. He had invited a few friends from university and the young woman to dine together that night, to meet his friend. They met at a *brasserie*, and no one ate, everyone drank. He noticed how his friend, standing amongst the group of his university friends, was looking at him. Her eyes were pleading. They were saying, *Let's go away, you and I, let's leave this place, your friends and your fiancée.* But then he was not in the mood, the same way she had not been in the mood to sleep with him a few months before when he had visited her. He grew annoyed. She saw it.

Later in the evening she fainted. One of his university friends caught her just before she fell to the floor. He believed she had feigned malaise to escape the place and the group and his fiancée. A friend said that it was hot and they had eaten nothing and drunk too much. But he got angry and, when she could feel her legs again, he said, 'Why don't you go back to your hotel?' And she left.

At his fiancée's place he could not sleep. He called her hotel several times. It had been late when his friend left for her hotel and there had been no public transport to take her there. He kept ringing her room until, early in the morning, she picked up.

'Where have you been?' he asked. She hung up.

He called again. She picked up straight away and said, 'I don't want anything to do with you.'

That was the end of their friendship.

He wrote to her several times, but she did not respond. He called her mother's place once, several years after the friendship had broken up, and her mother said that she had moved to Ireland. He got a telephone number from her. The mother had said that she would be pleased to hear from him, so one evening when he was rather tipsy, he called her in Ireland. She did sound pleased to hear from him. She told him that she was happy, although she gave no details. She only said that she was teaching French literature and that she had done a doctorate on Marguerite Duras.

After the phone call he wrote her a long letter, telling her what had happened between the young woman and him, why they had not got married, and how he had consequently been depressed. He talked about the other young women he had met since, how he had moved to Australia and how he was now occupying his days. His letter did not rekindle their friendship, as he had hoped; it had in fact the opposite effect. In response she wrote:

> *I had completely taken you out of my life, and believe me, it was not difficult. I had forgotten everything. I don't look back, that's how I am. I didn't suffer from your*

depression, which closely resembles an attempt to win back the attention of those who have given up on you.

I didn't answer your letters six years ago because I didn't see any purpose in doing so, and I didn't have the desire to.

I have no respect for you. Your letter in the form of a diary reminds me of a you I knew, egocentric and pedantic, whom I have no desire to meet again. Your stories do not interest me.

I do not want to be one of your memories. So, it's simple: forget me.

The letter was the burning of the temple. She had forgotten everything. If indeed she had succeeded in forgetting their friendship, it amounted to the destruction of something timeless and beautiful.

His wife had been right: he was slowly reading *The Old Capital*. After his bath, and before dinner, while his wife was writing postcards or dozing off, lying down on the tatami. He had decided not to read in the bath.

The young woman in the novel, Chieko, became their guide to Kyoto. So far, she had taken them to the Nishiki Market, the Botanical Garden and the Nishijin neighbourhood. The Nishijin of today didn't appear too different from the Nishijin of the 1960s, where a family from the novel owns a shop. The small shops lining the streets of Nishijin still belonged to weavers, and kimono and obi makers.

Each time he opened the book Chieko's face changed, depending on the young Japanese women he had seen in the streets.

Tonight the young woman was at the Gion Festival in Higashiyama and he said to his wife, who was sitting at the low table, legs crossed, and writing a postcard, 'Tomorrow, we'll go to Higashiyama.'

She said, 'Yes, it's on our list of things to do.'

The next day they went to Higashiyama and had a terrible row.

She had wanted to go by bicycle, which they did, though he thought walking would have been more practical. He had argued that the narrow, cobble-stoned streets of Ninen-zaka and Sannen-zaka could not be travelled up and down on bicycles. The guidebook, he pointed out, said it was a walking tour, not a cycling one. She had said, 'We'll see,' and they had gone by bicycle.

He became frustrated when they started cycling up the hill leading to the Kiyomizu temple. The hill was very steep, and he had to get off his bike to push it. In protest, he stopped by a cemetery by the narrow, deserted street, while his wife continued cycling up the hill. From halfway up the hill, at the cemetery, he enjoyed a clear view of the business district and the glass train station below.

He finally reached the top of the hill and the gate of the temple, with its large three-storey pagoda. Behind his wife, who had been waiting for him at the gate, hundreds of tourists were roaming the temple grounds, mostly in groups headed by guides with small flags on their caps.

He said, 'Where do you propose we park our bikes?' He was sweaty and out of breath.

'Over there,' she said, pointing to a magnolia tree near a small gate of the temple.

'I'm sure it's not allowed.'

She did not respond and went ahead. They parked the bikes under the tree.

They visited Kiyomizu without saying a word. The camera hung around his neck, but he took no photographs. She did not ask for the camera.

They cycled down the hill to Sannen-zaka on a

street busy with tourists walking up to Kiyomizu. As he had predicted, it was not an easy thing to ride on the cobble stones and through the crowd of tourists on foot, so he got off his bike and pushed. So did she, a little further on.

They pushed their bicycles into alleyways lined with small, ancient one or two-storey houses, some with skirt-roofs. Some were teahouses, where they did not stop, although they had planned to.

They arrived at Maruyama Kōen, and beneath a very old cherry tree he reproached his wife for being too bossy. They always had to do things, he said, the way she wanted them done. They had taken the bicycles, he continued, which was clearly a bad idea, and now they were burdened with them because she had not listened to him – she never listened to him. They had taken the bicycles because she decided to take them. Why couldn't she, occasionally, go along with how he thought things should be done?

He saw she was growing angry, which made him think that once more she was not listening to what he was saying. Had she been listening to him, she would have recognised that, yes, they almost always did things her way, and that rarely did they do things the way he suggested. In fact, he had practically stopped giving his opinion on how things could be done and mostly was happy to go along with her initiatives. Except today.

In a loud, angry voice she disagreed with what he had said, about her being bossy. He exaggerated. But to him, her position was not tenable – the bikes were a perfect example! After some time arguing, she walked away, pushing her bike. Riding a bike in the park was forbidden and, in truth, impractical.

The film director Yasujirō Ozu sometimes shows his characters' emotions in images of still life. In *Late Spring* a daughter asks her father a question. The father does not respond. During the silence Ozu shows a vase. When we see the daughter again, after a few moments, she is crying, and we, viewers, because of the stillness and simplicity of the vase we have just seen, are overwhelmed by the daughter's emotions. How would Ozu show his emotions? Perhaps by showing his bicycle resting against the trunk of the old tree, and then cutting to him gazing blankly at the flowers and tourists in the park.

They met again at the ryokan in the late afternoon. She was asleep on the mattress. He silently changed into his yukata and went down to the baths in the basement. The following day, although the anger had subsided, they did not talk much. It was as if they were tired and had no energy to make conversation. They stayed in the neighbourhood and visited a couple of small commercial art galleries and a teahouse. They slept most of the afternoon. He took his ritual bath around half past four, then they went out for an early dinner. The following morning they left Kyoto without having visited the Northern Mountains of Kitayama and their temples.

§

'Nara was the capital in the eighth century,' he said. 'Kyoto was the capital between the eleventh and nineteenth centuries.' He was now reading from the guidebook: '*…until the imperial restoration in 1868, when government functions were transferred to Edo. Edo then changed its name to Tokyo – meaning Capital of the East.*'

'Yes,' she said, uninterested.

'I wonder which city will be capital after Tokyo. Asuka was capital four times.'

She laughed.

'It won't be in our lifetime,' he continued. 'One rarely sees a country change capital during a lifetime.

Burma, though, changed its capital recently. To a place with an unpronounceable name in the middle of nowhere. The Great City of the Sun, they called it!'

'Capitals aren't designated like cities hosting the Olympic Games,' she said laughing a little.

He stopped talking and looked ahead as they walked towards the immense gate of the Tōdai-ji temple.

At about four in the afternoon, tired after a day of walking but unwilling to return to the ryokan just yet, they sat on a bench by a pond facing the pagoda of the Kōfuku-ji temple. His wife told him that since they had arrived in Japan a week ago, she had been constipated, and that even though she felt fine, she was getting worried. He suggested they look for a pharmacy.

They criss-crossed the lanes of the neighbourhood until they stumbled upon a small shop that resembled a pharmacy. They walked in. They had found a word for constipation in the phrasebook. '*Bempi*,' she said to a little old man who was watching a small TV placed on the counter, and she pointed at her stomach. He did not understand, so she showed the Japanese text for the word in the phrasebook – but the writing was too small, and despite having adjusted his reading glasses on his nose, the old man could not read it. She looked at her husband, helpless. 'Bempi,' he repeated. She followed suit: 'Yes, bempi!' Then both said 'bempi' in unison, several times, she pointing at her stomach, looking at the old man for a reaction.

At some point, without showing he had understood what they wanted, the old chemist went to the shelves behind his counter and picked up a small box, which he presented to them. The drawing with fluorescent colours of the digestive system on the front of the box gave his wife no doubt that the medicine was intended to help digestion. She turned the box and saw, in minuscule font and the Roman alphabet, a list of chemicals. She said to him that she preferred something herbal, that this was full of chemicals she had never heard of.

'Couldn't drinking more tea, or more of a certain type of tea, help?' he asked.

'Yes, perhaps,' she said.

She handed the box back to the pharmacist, and they both thanked him in English.

Once in their room, she ordered some ginger tea, and he changed into a yukata to go to the baths down in the basement.

The following morning they had their breakfast in the ryokan's small dining hall. A few Caucasian tourists were whispering over their miso soup, rolled omelettes and broiled fish, sitting cross-legged, or on their knees, or on their buttocks, legs folded to one side, on pillows on the tatami. Mid-breakfast, his wife took the room key off the table and excused herself.

§

Some places had stone baths, others wooden baths. The places with less character had tiled baths, like small, shallow swimming pools in the basement. He took daily baths when they came back from their day out visiting gardens, temples, museums, quaint neighbourhoods, markets. Time in the tiled baths in a steamy room lit with neon tubes brought him peace. Even when the baths were busy with shrivelled old men who became shy when he appeared, placing small towels over their private parts. No one ever spoke to him in the baths.

Bathing was not such an easy thing. In every bath the water was so hot that he withdrew his foot only a few seconds after dipping it in. His foot and the part of the lower leg that had been in the water would be pink, as if he were wearing a pink sock. Then he would lift the other leg over the side of the bath, enter it and sit on the submerged bench, holding his breath until his body told him the burning sensation was now bearable. The water bubbled here and there where hot spring water rushed into the bath or, as in the Dōgo Onsen, ran from a tap or pipe on the wall.

No one spoke to him in the baths, and that suited him. He thought Japanese men perceptive: they did not speak to him when he did not wish to be spoken to.

In the baths, he often thought of his aunt Edmonde. Of what she had told him about Japan. How he missed her letters, writing to her, and the prospect of visiting her! While in the baths, his mind saw her thin silhouette, and the pain etched on her face – the pain that struck that small body without warning, lingered, nearly faded, then struck again. The last time they saw each other, as they took the empty teacups to the kitchen, she had asked him to massage her back firmly; only after ten minutes of pushing up and down her back while she leaned against the bench did she tell him he could stop.

The morning was sunny, and he looked forward to the long day ahead. He was particularly looking forward to the *kabuki* theatre that evening. They took the metro from Asakusa to Otemachi, in Central Tokyo, where they were to visit the imperial gardens and a couple of museums nearby. Afterwards, they would wander about, looking out for interesting monuments and buildings, or smaller museums and galleries. He would also look out for bookshops where he could purchase the English translations of Japanese literature.

Mid-morning they went to the National Museum of Modern Art. It was earlier than they had planned but the imperial gardens happened to be closed that day.

The statue of a naked woman on the third floor was the second work of art to arouse him. The statue was life size. It was on a pedestal, so the woman was taller than he was; her mouth was level with his forehead. He could not tell whether she was Japanese. He looked around for his wife. He wanted to tell her something about the statue and ask her whether she thought the woman was Japanese or not. But his wife was not in the room. He was alone in the room.

He heard footsteps on the wooden floor in the adjacent room and a voice crackling on a walkie-talkie. Briskly, he leapt onto the pedestal. He was now behind the woman. He pressed his body against hers. She was not cold; she was firm, but with his clothes between his skin and her bronze, she did not feel cold. He moved his hands over her face and breasts and down her hips. He stepped off the pedestal and with his right hand pushed his erect penis hard against his lower stomach once or twice. He moved to a corner of the room. There stood another sculpture – a squirrel lying on its side.

At the kabuki theatre, they rented headsets that played commentary and translations of the songs and dialogue in English. The Japanese audience also wore headsets. The plays, the English commentary explained, were performed in old Japanese that the current generation could not fully understand.

He was amused to read in the programme that the female roles in kabuki were played by men. Somehow, that fact disappointed him.

The first play began with a tall, bulky samurai who strode past the audience on the ground floor of the theatre, roaring vengeful promises as he mounted the stage.

When, at the interval, the young woman sitting beyond the woman beside him stood up, he thought her very short. He thought he was twice as tall as she was. He also thought her of great beauty. As they stood near each other, stretching their legs, arms, and necks, he asked her in English whether she needed the headset's modern-Japanese translation to follow the dialogue and songs. In very good English she answered – smiling a seductive smile, he thought – that yes, she needed the translation to understand. The Japanese language of the plays was old and funny, she said, and although she understood some of it, she could not concentrate hard enough to make sense of all of it. Her grandparents perhaps would understand. Perhaps not. She asked him and his wife, now standing beside him, if it was their first time in Japan. Once they had answered, she introduced herself as Aska.

The commentary noted that the third act of the third play, *The Love Suicides at Sonezaki*, was regarded as one of the most poetic passages in Japanese literature.

The third act told of the journey of the young soy-sauce and oil merchant Tokubei and the geisha

Ohatsu to the world of spirits. It was lengthy and its beauty not so obvious to him. Although he appreciated that beautiful literature could come out of the predicament the two lovers found themselves in, they were taking an awfully long time to die.

The play was narrated by a group of musicians at the side of the stage whose singing he found comical and strange, but not beautiful. The singing reminded him of cats' meows. The music, however, did not bother him. The two actors in the third act, the suicide act, moved in slow motion in the Sonezaki forest, as if floating in the ether of death, even though they were not yet dead. Their initial admirable rashness was tempered by their slow motion and self-pitying diatribes.

Ohatsu mused at how they were both in their unlucky year: his twenty-fifth and her nineteenth. Tokubei expressed his concern about the lovers' looking ugly in death, and suggested they fasten their bodies to the twin-trunked tree nearby – to die 'immaculately', the commentary said.

In the end, by a palm tree to which Tokubei tied Ohatsu, the blade of the young merchant's dagger entered his lover's throat before he pressed it into his own.

After the play, they lingered in their seats, sharing their impressions of kabuki with Aska. She agreed with all they had to say. She said perhaps they already had plans, but she would be delighted if they joined her and a few friends for karaoke in Shinjuku the following evening. He and his wife tried to remember their plans for the following evening but could not. They said they would do whatever they had planned another time and accepted the invitation.

The next day, his wife did not feel well. Her stomach was acting up again, and she said she wouldn't go out that evening, so he went alone to meet Aska and her friends. After his bath, he changed from his corduroys and checked shirt into blue jeans and a black T-shirt.

In his early thirties he had read Tanizaki. He had started with the essay *In Praise of Shadows*, because it had been mentioned in a magazine article and its title intrigued him. He had been happy during his Tanizaki period: he had met his wife; he had read almost everything he could find in the English except Tanizaki's translations in modern Japanese of *The Tale of Genji*. He remembered the books very well. He had felt sorry for the men in Tanizaki's stories – the young and middle-aged husbands in *A Fool's Love* and *The Key* and the old diarist of *Diary of a Mad Old Man*, whose sexuality was pathetic.

He had sensed in *The Key* and *Diary* that the sensual desires inhabiting the middle-aged husband

and the old man – one could call these desires 'demons' insofar as they were lecherous and untameable – were those that had inhabited Tanizaki himself. Tanizaki was a middle-aged man when he wrote *The Key* and an old one when he wrote *Diary*.

During his readings of the novels he had understood these demons intellectually; he had recognised them from middle-aged and old men around him, particularly his father, but could not place them in the context of his own sexuality. He could not relate to them. How could a man satisfy a sensual desire with the sight of a woman's bare ankle or the sucking of one of her toes?

Tonight he wanted to touch Aska's skin. At first the skin of her hand would have been enough. But this urge grew and had now taken over him. And, like the old man in *Diary* who wanted to touch his daughter-in-law's foot, he now wanted to take Aska's foot, whichever one, in his hands and slowly run his fingers along its sole and top, rub it, and later perhaps, suck her big toe.

I am an aging fool, he thought. The desire for this young Japanese woman, who was singing and sometimes locking eyes with him and with the others, would not be tempered that evening and would not leave him for months after he had returned home. She stood up in the tiny cubic room and danced a little and displayed strange, most likely fashionable, dance moves while she and others sang. He wanted this room to belong to a brothel and Aska to a Madame he could pay to touch her foot and place his hands on her perfect hips and flat stomach, which sloped down towards her pubis in aesthetic perfection.

He wanted the liberty to do as he pleased with such beauty. He felt his aging had deprived him of this liberty, which he had on too few occasions taken when he was younger: the liberty to seduce, to play with sexuality, to be lecherous. In truth, the times he had played that game he had mostly failed, and suffered as a result, as he had in his thirties when he met the young and beautiful Younghee. Or, as with Hanna, he had travelled to places he later regretted having travelled to for they had only presented him with self-resentment and sadness, hers, but also his.

For now, he could not act as his desire dictated, or he would end up at the police station. Perhaps he could devise a strategy to touch Aska's skin, but to his complacent mind that was too intricate. What was now an obsession with her did not allow him to think, to calculate.

He was helpless and pathetic, as he had been when he was a teenager. But now he had passed the mid-point of his life, and he was convinced he would live the rest of it sexually helpless and pathetic, like Tanizaki's men.

He stayed until everyone was gone. Aska had been the first to leave, and he stayed with her friends, who sang while he slowly drank his beer. She had not touched him when she left; she had waved goodbye and smiled. 'I hope you enjoy the rest of your stay in Japan,' she had said across the small room. He had smiled back.

When he got back to the ryokan, he went down to the basement for a late bath. There he fell asleep for a while. He had fallen asleep pondering whether to go out again to find a beautiful prostitute or to watch a pornographic film at the theatre he had seen two blocks away. Although the violence of his desire for Aska had subsided, her face and small body, her narrow waist and perfectly round hips, were still before him. Her jeans had covered her hips, but her stomach, on occasion, had been exposed, depending on her dance moves or sitting position. He had seen her navel when she stood. It had looked, to him, like the first button to kiss and undo before those of her jeans fly. He had wanted to press his face against her pubis: through the denim first, then later against her hair and skin.

His skin was very red when he got out of the bath. He dried himself slowly – he had almost no energy left. Back in the bedroom, he slipped softly into bed beside his wife, under the duvet, which he soon pushed away because he was too hot.

At bus stops and in the metro corridors in Asakusa, he saw Kawabata's face on posters. 'That is Kawabata!' he said to his wife. They could not understand what the posters were about. But the face – the same photograph he had seen, in small format, on the back of *The Old Capital* and other Kawabata books he owned – was now as large as a tatami mat, and he could make out the lines marking Kawabata's skin. The photo was of Kawabata as an old man. His hair was like a white mane.

Why Kawabata's face was plastered across bus stops, metro stations, and corridors he did not know. The old man's face, in black and white, was from another time. It was anachronistic in its tranquillity and stillness.

He thought of a haiku he had recently read in the anthology of Japanese poetry he had bought in a central Tokyo bookshop. He now knew by heart several haikus in English translation. Haikus were short, and easy to memorise.

Lonely now –
Standing amidst the blossoms
Is a cypress tree.

The Rougon-Macquart Problem

When they returned from Japan, he finally unpacked the ink drawings by Henri Michaux his aunt Edmonde had left him.

Michaux's framed drawings now hung on the two walls of the upstairs corridor. His wife thought they should hang there. She said there was no other place for them. The corridor walls were bare. He thought they could have moved some of the paintings out of their living room and hung Michaux's drawings above the couch – they had been above a couch in the living room at Edmonde's – but he knew his wife would have refused. The drawings were not so bad where they were. He now looked at them every day when he went to his study and when he left it and when he went to bed and when he left the bedroom. His wife also saw them every day. They were most likely more prominent there, in the upstairs corridor, than downstairs above the couch. When one sits on the couch, one never looks above it.

The corridor had no windows, and the only light on the drawings came from two bulbs hidden in shades hanging from the ceiling. He first positioned the drawings so the light would fall at their centre. His wife criticised the positioning for not being centred on the walls. It looked strange, she said, to have them like this. He explained why he had positioned them as such. His wife said that they would look fine, even if the light did not reach each corner of a drawing more or less equally. Their dominant tone was grey, after all, she said, light need not illuminate them in a symmetrical manner to bring out their essence. He might even have discovered new details if the light shone more on some areas than others, which could have made him look at them in different ways than he was used to. She had a point, he thought. He said, true, but let's see how they go as they are; we can always reposition them later.

When he entered his study, he entered a 'room of his own'. That was how his wife now referred to it, a room of his own. He had been surprised when he first heard her refer to it as such.

What did he say to her then? Out of the blue – they were sitting on the couch watching the day's political report on television – he asked if she could imagine how long thirty-six years was.

'We haven't been married thirty-six years,' she said.

He smiled.

'No,' he said. 'I haven't completed a piece of writing in thirty-six years.'

'Yes,' she said. 'You did publish some stories when you were young, didn't you?'

'You know,' he said, 'our trip to Japan did something to me.'

She smiled. He thought she was going to mock him, but she said she had felt it did. He moved his gaze from the television to her face; she looked at him.

'Why don't you do something about it?' she said.

That was an expected phrase from her. How many times had she said to him, Why don't you do something about this, do something about that?

She didn't ask in what way the trip had affected him.

'I'm thinking of taking time off work. Indefinitely. I'm thinking of writing a novel based on Edmonde's life; I also have some ideas for a story about a couple in their fifties travelling to Japan…'

Her eyes were now on the television.

'You should do it,' she said.

He had expected an argument, but she agreed.

'Are you sure?' he asked. 'It will mean less income for us.'

'I think you should do this,' she said.

'I might refurbish the spare room,' he said. 'Get rid of the bed.'

'That's a good idea,' she said.

He set up the spare room as a study, with a new desk and a long, narrow teak table. And shelves. The long table stood against a wall, dedicated to his research, with the printer on it. The desk was placed under the window. From the window he looked over Alexandria's low rooftops and, farther away, over Surry Hills' housing estate, with its orange-brick walls, fifteen storeys tall, and countless square windows. Not the most picturesque view, but a view, a view of his own.

One evening, he was still in his study hunched over a large book of Japanese paintings when his wife discreetly came in. She looked around. She saw on the long table some of the photographs they had taken of the temples and gardens of Matsuyama, Kyoto and Tokyo, other open books, and pages in his handwriting. On the desk, his computer, some postcards of art works from museums, some standing, some lying, the topless woman from *In a Pensive Mood.* A black-and-white framed photograph of a young Edmonde.

'You have a room of your own,' she said.

He turned around on his swivel chair. She handed him a little book by Virginia Woolf, *A Room of One's Own*. He smiled at her.

He had the room; he had the time. The study – 'the study' is how he now called the room, the room of his own – was now his vantage point. Sometimes one looks back at one's life to search for memories and stories, to sift them for meaning, or rather for some recognition of oneself in them. If one is to perform such a search, one requires a revealing vantage point. He felt his study could be such a place. Not so much because of the change of furniture, the freedom to have mementos from his past – his postcards from museums, his photos, notes – scattered around, but because this physical space was to accommodate his solitude. For a long time now he had been inhabited by the need to be alone, to have little or no connection to others, to hold no responsibility.

His aunt Edmonde used the living room of her apartment. The small card table, its top covered with green felt. From there, she had smoked cigarettes and looked at a few years of her life, when she was in her late twenties and early thirties, the time she had with François and the few months after.

§

Émile Zola lived in the town of Médan, by the railway tracks of the Paris-to-Cherbourg line. Trains would pass and the house's windows would shake, the windows of his study, where he wrote every day. The tracks were at the bottom of the garden. Today, from the train, one can see a giant bust of Zola on a pedestal in the garden. He was ten or eleven when he visited Zola's house. There was no bust in the garden then.

When the train approached Médan, he had started to look out for Zola's house. He wondered if he would recognise the house, if there would be time to see it, for the train was travelling fast. Thanks to the incongruous bust, he fleetingly saw the house. The sighting was very brief; no memory of the school trip returned. That day in Zola's house did not come back to the forefront of his mind. No vivid recollection, no illuminating images of the place or of his school mates. Just the vague remembrance of having visited

Zola's house, when Zola did not matter to him.

He had taken the *métro* from Gare Saint-Lazare to Rue du Bac.

How long had it been since he had walked these streets? Now they were foreign to him. He had known these neighbourhoods like the pockets of his trousers when, as a student, he had walked them ceaselessly. It was only upon approaching Galerie Maeght that the neighbourhood took on a familiar look. Then he had instantly recognised the gallery and, little by little, what was around the gallery.

In a small brasserie two or three blocks away from the gallery he found his aunt, Edmonde, sitting on a moleskin banquette, a small cloud of smoke floating about her. He thought of a little bird, a little white bird, for his aunt wore white trousers and a white blouse, as she always did. She put her cigarette out. She got up and they embraced. She eased her strong embrace long after he was ready to sit down. They sat. He gave her the book wrapped in the Galerie Maeght's paper. She smiled and said thank you and leaned across the table to kiss him. With her two hands, she pulled his face towards hers and aimed her kiss at his mouth. Her lips pressed a little against his mouth and a little against his right cheek.

'It's strange: your father is my brother, but it is you I love,' she said, once she was sitting again.

She loved him, he believed, because she had just been 'reborn'. During what she called her 'death', she loved ghosts, she said. Today her love was once more borne onto the living.

'Someone calls me.'

That's what it is.

'From time to time.'

Yes?

'We speak. He speaks to me…'

'You detest the telephone!'

‘I detest speaking on the phone… I speak to him; he listens to me. He speaks to me. His voice does me good. We spend hours on the phone.’

‘Who is he?’

‘A man of a certain age. A friend. He has his own life, and I don’t ask him questions. You see, I erupt with joy when the phone rings. I always hope it’s him calling.’

Sometimes her brother – his father – called for news.

‘What do you want me to say to your father? He takes me for a mad woman. He thinks that I see vampires… He did not understand I was dead, so how do I tell him I have been born again? When he stops by to see me he says I look well. Your father is nice to me but he doesn’t understand me. Only you understand me and I know you love me.’

He pondered:

What are we talking about when we talk about

this kind of love? This man calls her and they speak on the phone. She lives again. Does it mean that she loves this man? Because she loves this man, she loves others, including me? She says I understand her. Don't I simply listen to her without saying a word? Do I *really* understand her? She says my letters show that I do understand her. In the letters, I do not make comments about what she says to me; and I do not bear judgement, that is true. Does this mean I understand her? Wouldn't understanding her mean knowing why she does this or that; for instance, why she was recently reborn? Knowing the reasons that led her to let herself 'die' in the first place? Or, on the other hand, wouldn't it mean not interpreting her actions, not attempting to make any sense of them? Not condemning or approving of them?

She unwrapped and opened the picture book on Miró he had bought at the gallery and leaned over the table again to kiss him. 'Thank you, you're lovely,' she said.

'How is Colette Dubreuil?' he asked after they started eating.

'As mean as ever.'

'Why do you stay with her? You don't need to work.'

'I'm curious. I want to see what she will do next. This woman is capable of unimaginable cruelty. It's fascinating to watch.'

'Does she treat you well?'

'She is losing her mind. She confuses or forgets things. She misplaces the files I prepare for her and asks me to prepare the same files again. I say, "Dear Colette, you already have that file, look again, the research is complete, where have you put it?" She says, "Edmonde, don't take me for a fool or some demented old woman, get the research done and give me a file." She thinks I'm dishonest with her. I now make copies of everything I prepare so I don't have to do everything twice,' she answered smiling.

This was the smile he had known since his childhood and of which he had often thought. The smile was the way her face lightened up and how she looked at him. And what she smiled about. She was in her late sixties and her smile, as it always had, made him believe a child was before him, and that he himself was a child again. His aunt's smile was a landmark in his emotive realm, akin to a pleasant memory which never dissipated and regenerated itself each time they saw each other.

'But you know, what's really fascinating is what she's doing to her family, especially to her children. She's most cruel to her children. She is little by little, methodically, making sure they will receive nothing of her estate when she dies. She seems to be in possession of all her faculties when she wants to play dirty tricks…'

'What is she working on?'

'She is writing a book on Pechkoff.'

She seemed to expect that he knew who Pechkoff was.

'It's a fictionalised account of a Zinovi Pechkoff's life… He was the most charming of men, you know. Delicate, softly spoken. His French had such a beautiful accent, almost imperceptible, soft. His grammar was impeccable. I used to call him my "suave Legionnaire". He was handsome. He was one those people everyone seemed to like, to be drawn to.'

This was precisely what he wished people to say about him, that he was one of those people liked by everyone, everyone was drawn to…

'Will she complete the book before she dies?' he asked.

'No. She has only written a third and is working more and more slowly.'

'Are you writing her book?' he decided to ask.

She smiled while cutting a piece of her duck breast, she didn't look up at him, nor did she answer.

'Has your taste for Zola changed?' he asked later, telling her his train had passed by Zola's house in Médan.

'I suppose it has,' she answered, 'but I cannot read him in the *Pléiades* editions anymore. Do you enjoy these books? The pages are of this cigarette paper I find unpleasant to touch. The publisher has managed to cram Zola's works into three volumes made of that thin paper. With hundreds of pages of annotations, notes and commentary… I don't think I will read Zola again. I read him at about the time I met François…'

'I'm reading *L'Assommoir*. My first Zola.'

It was a rainy Saturday morning. Two or three weekends earlier at home in Sydney. He had walked to the bus stop and observed for the first time that two of his umbrella spokes were broken and that the umbrella's fabric was flapping in the rain where the spokes were broken. He waited over forty-five minutes for the bus. The 9.56 did not pass and he took the 10.16. Downtown the owner of the French bookstore warmly greeted him when he entered the small shop. There, over a coffee the owner had prepared at the back of the shop, they spoke for a while about how the book business was doing. He bought *L'Assommoir*, then got back on the bus, where he started reading the book. It was an old G. Charpentier edition but in good condition.

'I will read them all,' he said to Edmonde.

About six or seven years before he had read all of Stendhal. Edmonde had been thrilled when he told her in one of his usually short letters, as Stendhal was one of her favourite writers, but their conversation about Stendhal had been short when they met.

He found then that he could not talk about books. Not like Edmonde did. He could say that he had or had not enjoyed a book and had or had not finished reading it but he could not provide any sort of analysis. Characters, scenes, plots often lingered in his mind when he was reading and after he had read a novel, yet he did not think past these things. He did not see and therefore did not think about how it was written, or what else it might have said beyond what was printed on the pages. He did not think about the author's personality or craft. He used to, when he was young and started reading and writing, but he had not for a very long time.

A few weeks after he told Edmonde that he had read Stendhal, he received a postcard of a portrait of Stendhal painted by Dedreux-Dorcy, from the Musée Stendhal in Grenoble. Stendhal, gazing a little to his right, not at the painter, smiled almost imperceptibly. His forehead was high; the distance between the top of his nose and his hairline was roughly the same as between the bottom of his chin to the top of his nose. His head was surrounded by dark-brown hair; his moustacheless, collar-like beard seemed of the same short, wavy hair as of the top of the head. Although Stendhal looked serious in the painting, because of the imperceptible grin, he had seen bonhomie in the writer's face. He got the postcard framed and placed it on the bookshelf in the spare room.

They had drunk a bottle of Burgundy pinot with their lunch. He said he was happy with what he had eaten and drunk. It was good to eat the food and drink the wine he could not eat and drink every day in Sydney.

She now had to get back to Madame Dubreuil's and he walked her there. They kissed goodbye in front of the *porte cochère* of the building where Colette Dubreuil had her office. They didn't know when they would see each other again. It had been five or six years since they had last seen each other. He never knew when he would next be in France and when next in France if he would be able to come to Paris to see her. That was what he said to his aunt. So, she gave him a long and tight embrace. He then waited to see if, with her small build, she would succeed in pushing the large and heavy right-hand door of the porte cochère. As she lifted her right foot to pass the bottom part of the frame of the door, she turned back in his direction and smiled at him looking at her disappear.

§

A few years before that visit to France, he and his wife had spent a few days at his parents' house in Normandy, on their way to London, where his wife had to travel for work. His parents had gathered the extended family one evening.

He had hoped to sit next to his nephew's girlfriend at dinner. He could not help looking at her the first time he met her, the previous year. He sensed that, somehow, he and she had connected. At the *apéritif*, she had spoken to him more than to the other family members. On the couch they had sat on either side of his nephew, talking almost as if ignoring his presence between them. She told him about the acting classes she took during the university breaks, at the Cours Florent, where she had attended master-classes with Francis Huster and Vincent Lindon, and where she met Jean-Louis Trintignant. They had spoken about movies. She liked older movies, those where Trintignant was young.

He had tried to talk about literature with her, but she didn't seem to read much. Then the apéritif was over, and everyone was ushered by his mother to the dinner table. He was seated away from her. On a couple of occasions over dinner, their gazes met and they smiled at each other. She was sitting next to his nephew on one side and the host – his father – on the other, at the head of the table, and he had observed that she and his nephew often held hands under the table and whispered to each other from time to time.

His father had started conversations with her on several occasions but could not sustain one. He had made jokes that grew louder and cruder as the dinner went on. As he caught parts of the jokes his father was dispensing, he imagined his nephew's girlfriend must have been embarrassed by their vulgarity, but when he looked at her, she smiled at his father with what he took for a polite smile. He had seen no sign of disgust or embarrassment behind that smile – though she hadn't laughed. And yet his father somehow felt encouraged, perhaps by the apéritif's whiskies and the wine he was now drinking, and went on with the jokes.

That evening at his parents' house in Normandy, Edmonde was absent, for she rarely attended family gatherings; she disliked gatherings of more than two people.

His wife, as usual, struggled with the conversations in French, and he stayed by her side to interpret what she did not understand or wanted to say. She would get annoyed with him when he left her alone with his family members, none of whom spoke English. She would get frustrated when she could not contribute to a conversation. But he had never reproached her for not learning French. His wife was argumentative and would have had many rows, particularly with his father, had she been fluent in French.

In the absence of open communication between his wife and his parents, his parents' default attitude towards her was one of warm politeness – far from the warmth they extended to his brother's French wife, whom they saw regularly. And of course, he and his wife were childless. His parents, he knows, resent his wife, not him, for not having given them grandchildren, although it was he and his wife, the two of them, who decided not to have children. He had explained many times, when he and his wife were younger, that the decision had been mutual, but his parents, he knows, believed that their son came to the decision to be childless because of his wife's influence, that it had been her decision in the first place and that he had been led to agree to it.

His nephew's girlfriend's auburn hair was longer now. She had worn her hair short the previous year; now it fell almost to her shoulders. She was wearing a light summer dress. He took his wife to her at the apéritif, as his nephew's girlfriend spoke English well.

When she saw him, she smiled and said, 'How are you? Long time, no see!' She seemed to have grown in confidence, he thought, as he heard her voice say those words.

'Yes,' he said, 'long time, no see. This is my wife.' His wife introduced herself, and she and his nephew's girlfriend began talking about his wife's native country, while he and his nephew discussed the year just gone.

His nephew's girlfriend and his wife talked throughout the apéritif. His wife was aware that his nephew's girlfriend was most probably the only person who could speak English, and she wouldn't let the young woman talk to others.

They moved to the dinner table. The previous year his nephew's girlfriend had sat next to his father, and so she did again this year. She and his father seemed to have grown closer. They spoke and smiled at each other. His nephew, however, no longer sat beside his girlfriend but beside his mother and him.

At dinner he learned from his nephew that, the

previous summer, he and his girlfriend had spent a month with his parents at the house they rented each year in Bormes-les-Mimosas, in the south of France. They went to the beach together and often dined out. They visited Saint-Tropez and Le Lavandou. They played *pétanque* and cooked meat and fish on the barbecue. They snorkelled.

He pictured his father puffing out his white-haired chest, walking along the beach in his small swimming trunks, running into the water and diving through the waves, as he used to when he was a young man.

'How did you get on?' he asked his nephew.

'Well enough,' he said with a wry smile.

'How did she get on with them?' What he really wanted to know was how she got on with his father.

'You know Grand-Papa, especially after a few drinks, he has to be reined in.'

'Jesus!'

'But nothing major happened. She likes him. No drama. We had a good time.'

There is a painting at the Musée des Beaux-Arts in Angers called *Unequal Love.* He and Edmonde had gone to Angers several years earlier to call on his brother and visit the local museums. It is a Flemish-inspired work by an anonymous 19th-century artist. It is modelled on Quentin Matsys's *Ill-Matched Lovers.* It depicts a young and beautiful woman – beautiful by the canons of her own epoch, most likely the 16th century, not that of the painter. Perhaps she is a maid, or even a *fille de joie*; she sits at a table in an inn. At a large wooden table. Next to her, on her left, our right, sits an old man whose face is turned slightly towards her, as if leaning in, demanding an answer, perhaps harassing her. His ugliness is grotesque, unreal, like a mask from a satirical play. No one has ever had such a face. The ugliness painted into the old man's face made him think the old man's thoughts towards the young woman were equally absurd and ugly – unbearable to contemplate, like his face…

He is reminded of this painting as he recalls that dinner, his father and his nephew's twenty-year-old girlfriend sitting beside him. His father was rather handsome; he still is, in old age. Back then he sometimes glimpsed an underlying ugliness in him, though. What was it? Vulgarity? Spoken lechery when faced with beauty? Could someone have seen the same ugliness in himself when he had been confronted with Aska's beauty in Tokyo?

§

Yannick Berl and Jean Lucien, after Berl's death, had hired Edmonde as their private secretary.

Berl had asked her to lie, naked, on his desk while he worked. She refused, she told him. With that smile.

Lucien had told her that when he met young female readers he wore tight trousers and no underwear. Her smile.

Despite having known both writers intimately, she admired them.

When Lucien committed suicide at the end of 2000, aged eighty-one – he had told all his friends and acquaintances that he did not wish to live in the twenty-first century – she went to work for Colette Dubreuil.

Why his aunt was working for the unpleasant Dubreuil, at her age and now that she had been diagnosed with lung cancer, he could not fathom, though perhaps, somehow, he could.

One of his favourite jokes with her was that she had written most of Lucien's and Berl's books and was now writing Dubreuil's.

He was convinced, although he never raised it in all seriousness, that she might not have written

Lucien's and Berl's books but was indeed writing Dubreuil's book on Pechkoff.

His wife had been furious with him when he returned to Australia after his last trip to France and visit to Edmonde, he now told her. He had got it into his head to find and acquire a first edition of *Introduction à la médecine expérimentale* de Claude Bernard, the book that had inspired Zola to develop his notion of the naturalist novel, set out in the essays of *Le Roman expérimental.*

He had telephoned antiquarian bookshops in Paris from his parents' house until Bruno Cassini of the Librairie Ancienne Bruno Cassini, Rue Cassette, confirmed that he had the book. After a few calls, he had come to believe his search would lead nowhere. He enjoyed busying himself with such a project while at his parents'; it rescued him from the pathetic indolence he found himself in when visiting them, and he thought his quixotic quest a good story to write, should he ever decide and find the time to write a story.

He took the train to Paris, then the métro to Saint-Sulpice, rang the bell at Cassini's shop, which was locked like a bank vault because, he figured, of the value of the books it kept on its shelves. The shop smelt of attics. The book was in poor condition, and Cassini advised him to open it rarely and to use white cotton gloves when turning the pages. It was a large book, one you could not carry like a new book bought at your corner bookshop. In the back of his shop Cassini prepared a cardboard box for it while, at a distance, he looked at the shelves.

'Please refrain from touching any of the books,' Cassini had said with a polite expression before disappearing to the back of the shop.

As he waited, he began to regret buying the book. It was a very, very expensive object, one for which he had no use and no place. His wife would be furious at the expense, which amounted to the cost of a holiday for two, say in Japan. His wife yelled at him as soon as he set foot through the door; she had seen the credit-card debit on the statement before he returned to Australia: 'What were you thinking?! Do you know how much your book cost?'

'Yes,' he said.

'So? What are you going to do now? Sell it? Why don't you get your money back from the bookshop and send the book back?'

'He doesn't want the book back.'

He had called Cassini before leaving France, having changed his mind about the book. Cassini would not take the book back but said he would contact him if someone miraculously enquired after it. This was very unlikely, Cassini had warned repeatedly; he had been the only person who had ever approached him for the book. He had asked Cassini to let his regular clients know the book was for sale again. 'No,' the rare-books seller had said, 'this is not how I work.'

As he spoke to his aunt a year or so later, he was still looking for a way to get rid of the book and get the thousands of francs back. She laughed. Despite himself, he had hoped she might offer a solution, but she had none, of course, although he didn't openly seek her advice. He didn't wish to bring up money matters with her. The story was about the book, not money.

Later, at home, he wrote to his aunt on the back of a postcard showing a Howard Arkley painting:

When leaving your apartment the other day, I passed a couple and their two children in the street. I had passed them at almost the same spot on my way to see you.

Then he added, as a sort of postscript:

(Two children! Can you imagine it? Two children!)

§

How had he heard about it? It was not his nephew's girlfriend; it was not his nephew. Could it have been his mother? Perhaps, but most likely not. But who else could it have been? He remembers his outrage, and still feels embarrassed by it.

He was furious, although he knew it was none of his business. He had no role to play in the incident.

Was it an incident? Was it an incident because to him it was an incident? Was it an incident to anyone else involved? It was not. To everyone else it was a joke, and he found that fact disturbing – for to him the event had constituted an incident.

He can remember a long list of such incidents caused by his father. They seldom occurred in his presence – he was rarely there – but there was a history of such behaviour. What his father did didn't surprise him.

So, while exerting his usual effort not to argue with his parents during his latest stay, he heard of this and decided to say nothing, though, in his mind, the incident should have been discussed with them.

Two or three days into his stay, his brother and sister-in-law came to his parents' house to see him. They had lunch, preceded by a long and jovial apéritif, and dinner, preceded by another equally long and jovial apéritif.

And at dinner – why? During the apéritif, as they had talked about his parents' holidays in the south and his father's jokes had grown ever more vulgar, the pieces of an argument had begun assembling in his mind, like an army forming before battle – he said, in response to one of his father's jokes about breasts: 'Jesus, Papa! With you it always has to be about tits and arse. Can't we have a break from the crassness once in a while – from the same dirty old jokes, and from the touching of young women's breasts … while I'm at it.'

His father's expression changed instantly from amused to vexed.

'Yes,' he continued coldly, 'it is not acceptable that you grasp your grandson's girlfriend's breasts – at the dinner table or anywhere. Even on holiday. Even if she's only wearing a bikini top and a sarong, and everyone has been talking about breasts. Even if it seems to you a funny thing to do! What world do you think you're living in?'

His father now looked at him with fury in his eyes. In that gaze he also saw sadness. The sadness of having been betrayed? His father threw a glance at his mother.

Then his response arrived, after he had, or perhaps had not, collected his thoughts.

His father, in his authoritative tone, said that he rarely visited but, when he did, had to start arguments, that he had met his grandson's girlfriend only once or twice and didn't know her; that she hadn't been bothered by the gesture – she had laughed at the time, hadn't complained, it had been affectionate, not sexual, everyone knew that – it had been a joke, and why was he bringing it up now, with his brother and sister-in-law – his nephew's parents – present; and finally, why couldn't he come down from his high moral ground *while he was at it.*

He said, 'You know, Papa, there comes a time in a man's life when his parents no longer educate him, when it is he who must begin to educate them. I think we've reached that time.'

His father said nothing. Nor did anyone else at the table.

A little later, while he was talking with his brother and sister-in-law about their house renovations, his father rose to help his mother carry the dessert plates to the kitchen and didn't return to the table.

§

Once again, a year or so had passed since they had last seen each other.

They sat in her apartment; today she was not working. They sat on the couches beneath framed drawings by Henri Michaux and beside the bookshelves filled with art and picture books. On the large square coffee table, between piles of books, stood their two cups of Lapsang Souchong tea and *pâtisseries* from Lenôtre.

'It's good to be with someone who appreciates silence,' she said. 'Most people are uncomfortable when there's a moment of silence and feel that they have to break it. Not you.'

He had often kept silences between them because he had not known what to say to Edmonde. And, in those silences, he had often thought of her book. He had thought about what he might say, or about what they had just discussed, yet more often than not he thought of the book. The book they had never discussed. And how he could broach or if he should broach the subject of the book with her at all. She had never brought it up, so why should he? That was what he thought during the silences between them over the past thirty years. Since he first read the book.

A year or two after he had begun reading novels – he was perhaps nineteen or twenty – he found a new book titled *Hostal Frontera* in his local library. It was an erotic novel written by Lucia C. He had borrowed it because of the author's name – Lucia. Edmonde had had a friend called Lucia. He recalled a photograph of a beautiful woman, with large dark eyes, shoulder-length hair and a fringe, pinned on the wall of his aunt's bedroom when he first visited her, aged twelve. There was no photo or biography of Lucia C in the book. It did not say when or where she was born, where she lived, or whether she had written anything else. There was nothing about her, apart from her first name and the first letter of her last name. The novel had been published by a new Parisian publishing house. He figured it had been written in French, as there was no mention of a translation or translator. It was a short book, and to him a beautifully written one.

The book told of a love triangle between the narrator – seventeen-year-old Lucia – and a French couple in their thirties, Edmonde and François. The novel was very detailed when it came to love scenes and dreams. For the first two-thirds the story took place in Santiago, Chile. The final third told of a lonely Edmonde in her Paris apartment, after François's death, surrounded by her memories of him and Lucia and by her fantasies. The book finished with the visit of Edmonde's twelve-year old nephew. The final chapter told of their visits to museums and their nascent relationship.

He had been tremendously aroused by the book

– practically at every page. He had been excited by Lucia, François, Edmonde and the nameless nephew's sexual feelings and acts. He was the nephew. He had, of course, realised after a few pages that Edmonde had written the book. He remembered the notebooks he had opened in her apartment during that first stay with her. That was where she had written the book, in those notebooks, on the small square card-table.

The book became well known. Literary circles had talked a great deal about it and speculated endlessly about who Lucia C was, agreeing that the name was a pseudonym. His aunt's name never surfaced. The authorship of *Hostal Frontera* has, to this day, remained a mystery.

A few weeks after reading the book, he thought he was probably the only person, apart from the publisher, perhaps, who knew who Lucia C really was. His parents might have recognised people and places in the book and deduced that Edmonde had written it, but they did not read novels and he was not going to tell them about the book.

Lucia C herself might have realised that Edmonde was the author, had she ever heard of or read the book. But who was the real Lucia C, where did she live? The book was later translated into many languages, and she might have read it in one of them…

He had read it many times and found it a landmark in his sexual life. The scenes in the book had the sharpness of vivid memories. The book had always aroused him; every time he opened it, he knew he would masturbate. Often he opened it for that purpose, as an adolescent might open a *Lui* magazine to find sexually wired images. He had read passages to lovers.

But he never asked his aunt about the book. She knew he read a lot and perhaps she knew by instinct that he knew about the book. But they never discussed it.

Because of the book, he had often pondered his aunt's sexuality. It seemed to him that, after François's death, and for a long while, Edmonde's sexuality drew its inspiration from her husband's absence and was limited to memories of François and Lucia, and to dreams of men and of a man's touch. And to sex in her book, and perhaps in other books and artworks.

Wasn't what she had called her 'death' François's absence?

At present, she talked to him about her lovers. It started with the man of a certain age who called. He no longer called, but others did, and they visited her. Who were her lovers? Were they men in their early seventies too? Younger men? She talked about her lovers. She said her doctors were surprised she had lovers. And she talked about lovers, not *a* lover. How many men was she seeing?

She said her gynaecologist had saved her sexuality.

'He said to me years ago, after François's death: "If you ignore your vagina, it will dry out, shrink, and wilt; you must keep it alive by stimulating it, you must look after it." "I come to see you," I said. "Isn't that looking after it?" "Yes," he said, "but you must also listen to me, Edmonde, and follow my advice. If you won't have sexual intercourse with anyone, then masturbate at the very least. Use lubricants if you have to, but masturbate – masturbate constantly. It will keep your vagina in good health, and if – God forbid," he said, smiling – "you ever decide to fuck again, you may find pleasure once more." And he was right, the darling.'

He had often longed to talk to his aunt about his sexuality. More so when he was much younger, and acutely a few years after he had married.

Back then he and his wife did not make love much. He had wanted to say to his aunt: she and

I are young, yet our sexual relations are scarce and conventional. He preferred masturbating to making love to his wife and, paradoxically, she was often the main female protagonist in the erotic scenarios he constructed when masturbating.

But he never said anything to his aunt on the subject.

As she had when he was young, she asked him about his sex life at each visit. She would ask, with her smile, '*Et le cul ?*' He could not think of a literal translation in English. It was a phrase he might have expected from his father – though his father had never asked him about his sex life – yet, emanating from her small figure, dressed in a crisp white suit, uttered in her frail voice as she looked into him with that smile, it almost sounded absurd.

He knew he gave pitiful answers, when he gave answers at all, pitiful in their vagueness and disappointing to Edmonde. But his aunt never insisted, never probed, and always closed the conversation, the conversation about the sex life they did not have, with a smile.

What bothered him then was not so much the lack of sexual relations, or their conventionality, but that in the end he was not bothered by their infrequency and conventionality. He felt he should have. He was also concerned that his wife might grow anxious about the tepidness of their sex life. He was not afraid she might leave him, but feared that something would make her deeply unhappy, for he felt that the lack of sex could make a person profoundly unhappy.

Answering his aunt's question or bringing the subject up with his wife could have led to the beginning of a resolution, or to answers to some of the questions. But how to discuss such questions?

And he had been unsure as to what to admit to his wife. Where did his responsibility lie? In bed, before sleeping, he was happy to leave his wife alone and read. But he didn't know, and therefore could not explain, why. Some things, he thought then, cannot be explained – they simply are. A table is a table and a chair is a chair; one cannot explain why.

§

In the book, Edmonde and François stay at the Hostal Frontera in Santiago. This is how the book starts. They have just arrived at the hotel and are arguing about where to put their things. They have more clothes, books, and magazines than the room can hold. Yet they like the hotel: the spring air of its inner courtyard, the swallows nesting in the arched hallways, its bar – they are excited to be away from home, and, perhaps because their spirits are high and their bodies tired, they quarrel and will soon make love.

That evening, after a light dinner with local wine, they go to bed, each in a single bed. Their beds are only separated by the width of a bedside table and they hold hands.

Then Lucia C tells of Edmonde and François's meeting. The first of the three chapters deals mostly with their respective sex lives up to their meeting. Their first sexual experience occurs within an hour of meeting, on a bench in the Jardin du Luxembourg, after they first meet at a reception in the Senate. Their sexualities, as portrayed by Lucia C, are unbridled, wide and profound. Their sexual desires are the reference point for every decision they make; their fulfilment, their cardinal ambition. Later, they will spend several years of their lives in Chile because the bright object of their sexual desires, the young Lucia C, lives in Santiago. The second chapter tells of the French couple's immersion in the Chilean culture, their friendships with artists and writers, and their monomania for Lucia. In the final chapter, after several years at the Hostal Frontera, François dies of syphilis; Edmonde's sexual urges fade and she returns to their Paris apartment.

On the table, two boxes from the *pâtisserie* Lenôtre lay open. One held macaroons of various colours, the other chocolate éclairs. Edmonde made tea. The familiar scent of Lapsang Souchong drifted from the spout of the teapot on the table. There were also two port glasses and a bottle of port, which she opened and poured into the glasses. She lit a cigarette.

He had visited Edmonde many times, yet that day, for the first time, he realised how little had changed in the apartment since his first visit over thirty years earlier. Ever since, the same ritual had marked his visits, and the thought that it might soon end plunged him into quiet melancholy.

His parents had told him he would find her cadaverous, as they had when they last called on her. He did not; he was annoyed by their morbid choice of word. He found her slightly emaciated.

She told him about the medication she had to take. She told her specialist she did not want aggressive treatment; she did not want to lose her hair or have the medication make her ill. So she was undergoing a mild treatment, which still gave her stomach cramps, muscle pain, and nausea. She was in pain.

'You know, I've had to change doctors several times. They've been unbearable. They tell me to stop smoking. I've smoked all my life; I'm not going to stop now, am I? They're so patronising. I told them: I'm seventy-four; don't speak to me as if I were an adolescent, but they can't help themselves. My current doctor is more reasonable: he listens, and he's stopped nagging me about the smoking.'

He agreed with her perspective. Why should she stop smoking now? He always agreed with her; he always came to see things from her perspective.

'Dubreuil's book?' he asked.

She smiled.

'I'll have to finish Colette's book,' she said. Silence.

'The poor woman is now rewriting chapters we completed last year,' she went on pensively. 'As she rewrites them, they become increasingly melancholic, and, I find, more beautiful. She has rewritten scenes in which Pechkoff argues with his brother about Lenin, and they made me weep. Colette gives Pechkoff a cruel side. In these scenes he harshly judges Lenin's and his brother's low intellect and tells his brother that he and Lenin are as stupid as their father, the coppersmith, was. When they were young, he and his brother mocked their father, who was illiterate and naïve. She's given him a pessimistic side too: he dooms the socialist dream before it even begins, although some of its philosophy appeals to him. I wept when I typed those pages. She doesn't remember she's already written these scenes, these chapters, but I let her rewrite them because her writing is reaching a purity and a truth I've not seen in her previous work…'

She paused to draw on her cigarette.

Then: 'Her children, and some of her grandchildren, are suing her, but she doesn't seem to realise. She no longer answers calls from her lawyer, who's in a panic and rings her doorbell every other day. She tells me to tell him she doesn't want to see him, that she's busy writing, that he's failed her, since she's being sued by everyone she knows, but she couldn't care less about being sued…

'She writes about people, the kind she wishes there were more of, the kind she says have vanished. Today, she says, people have it too easy; manners, dignity, and courage have gone with the bathwater. People can't speak or write French properly any more. They can all go to hell with her money – and that includes me. "Take my money, Edmonde, since you so desperately want it! Why else would you be with me if you didn't want my money?" she says. "Because, *chère* Colette," I tell her, "if I'm not with you, who will be? You know perfectly well I'm only after your charming company." Then she shoos me out of her office.'

'Does she know about your condition?'

'She says I'm lying, that I'm not ill.'

She confided that she had been thinking a great deal about Jean Lucien.

Lucien had lived through both world wars and had been in the Resistance during the second. He was received at the Académie Française, at Fernand Braudel's chair, and still enjoyed reading Zola when he took his own life.

His first wife had died of cancer several months before and, even though they had been separated for four decades, he could not imagine himself in a world where she no longer was.

'What about the date?' he asked. 'The thirtieth of December 2000! And when did his wife die? In May that year, months before he did?'

She smiled. He had been talking about suicide for years, she said. Ageing frightened him; illness frightened him. The thought of senility, of being unable to read or write, terrified him. She and Lucien had often joked about how he might kill himself. Once, they had even considered his jumping from a plane without opening the parachute – Lucien had parachuted many times – but, she said, some well-intentioned companion would have floated over and opened it for him. The press would have concluded that either the parachute had been faulty or someone had sabotaged it to murder the old *académicien*. An inquiry would have been launched, wasting everyone's time. They invented a series of suicide scenarios, laughing at each, and, of course, never enacting any of them.

When Lucien's first wife fell ill, their discussions about suicide became less humorous and more practical. The illness quickly evolved and was diagnosed as terminal. Clearly his first wife's condition had changed Lucien's state of mind. He began inquiring about medication that could 'put him to sleep'. He knew he lacked the strength to jump from a plane, a building, or in front of a metro, and he did not wish to disfigure his body or expose his death to strangers. His death would have to be a private act, at home.

As if her thoughts had returned to those early, droll suicide scenarios, she said, 'Lucien had an incredible sense of humour...'

That was something he would have liked people to say about him – that he had an incredible sense of humour.

Lucien had always refused to read *Le Docteur Pascal*, because in it Pascal Rougon, his favourite protagonist in the *Rougon-Macquart* saga, dies. He could not bring himself to read Pascal Rougon's final moments, although he knew from others how he died. All his life, even though he knew he would find enormous pleasure in reading his last Zola, he neither owned nor opened a copy of *Le Docteur Pascal*.

As Lucien's talk of suicide grew more thoughtful, more practical, Edmonde offered to go to Librairie Castel, near the restaurant where they lunched, and buy him a copy of *Le Docteur Pascal*. After she had insisted over their next two or three lunches, Lucien finally accepted her offer – the end of the year 2000, the dawn of the new century, the new millennium, was only a fortnight away, she had reminded him – and she went to buy him *Le Docteur Pascal*.

A day or two later Lucien phoned to tell her how moved he'd been by the book – how wonderful it was to be again with his friend *le bon Docteur*. Docteur Pascal had now died, and his work on heredity had been destroyed by his mother; he had died alone; but he had died knowing that his love, his niece Clotilde, bore his child. By ending the *Rougon-Macquart* cycle with the birth of Pascal and Clotilde's child, the good Zola had completed it with optimism for the family's future. What a marvellous conclusion! Lucien had said to Edmonde.

When she heard of his death, Lucien's current wife, then in New York, jumped from her hotel window. She survived, spending two months in a U.S. hospital. Seven months later, she wheeled her wheelchair to the window of her Paris apartment and jumped again. This time she died – instantly.

The questions he wanted to ask Edmonde now that she had told him all this, three questions in fact, were: Do you want to decide when you die? If so, when? And do you wish me to help you?

Nothing was said for a while. He looked at the books lining the shelves behind his aunt, sipped his port, and thought he glimpsed some of Lucien's books, though he could not trust his eyesight.

Memory is a funny thing, he remembers saying to her. The compelling necessity to look back, to want to remember as if one were there again, to remember as if living it a second time. When I was a young man I looked forward. I wished then to know what sort of man I would be in the future. I remember the first day back at school after the Christmas holidays, when the teacher wrote the year on the blackboard. It was 1981. I remember the teacher very well, Madame Constantini, with her long, curly auburn hair. At that moment, as she wrote the new year's date, I wondered what I would be like in the year 2000. I had quickly calculated my age in 2000. What job would I have? I pictured myself, like Papa, in a three-piece suit, coming home after work, opening a briefcase full of papers, and taking out a packet of cigarettes to smoke with a whisky. The year 2000 is now far behind me.

I look backward now, he thinks he said to Edmonde. I think about the young man I was, even the child I was, the people I knew, what I did when I was seventeen, twenty, thirty, etc.

He asked her to play Berlioz's *Harold en Italie*. It was the first piece by Berlioz he had ever heard, over thirty years earlier, in the same apartment, after a visit to the Musée de l'Orangerie, where they had admired Utrillo's painting of Berlioz's house in Montmartre.

'How did Lucien die?' The question escaped before he could weigh its impact on Edmonde.

'He didn't want anyone to know how he died. The last time we saw each other, we agreed I would call every morning at eleven. There were only five or six days left in the year. The day he didn't answer, I would know he was dead and go to his flat to call the police. He'd asked me not to reveal the manner of his death.

He even left a note to that effect on his desk. I called the police, I called his wife. I couldn't tell her how he'd died. All I was allowed to say was that he had taken his own life. She understood.'

He told her later he was thinking of visiting Japan within the next year or two. She told him François had taken her to Kyoto when they had just met, and that the temples and gardens there were the most beautiful things she had ever seen. He smiled. He had never called anything 'the most beautiful thing he had seen'.

'I wish we were going together,' she said. 'I'd love to see them again, with you.'

He was alone in the room. On the table where she once wrote, there were now hundreds of minuscule pieces of a jigsaw puzzle. Edmonde had begun to sort them by tones of colour, into little piles. On the cover of the box was a picture of *The Rape of the Sabine*

Women by Poussin. This was the table where she read Zola, he presumed, smiling to himself – had she not once said that one could not read Zola in bed or on the train, that one had to read him at a table? – where she had written her book.

She came back from her bedroom holding an old, almost square briefcase of reddish-brown leather, with dark brown metal corners and latches on either side of the handle.

'I have been keeping this for you,' she said. 'It was Lucien's.'

In the apartment's red-walled anteroom, she placed her hands on his cheeks and gently drew his face towards hers. She kissed him close to the mouth, then again on the other side, a longer kiss. She did not loosen her grasp; she stared into his eyes. He did not move. He thought of pulling away, a reflex, but didn't. He looked into her eyes. He didn't wish to disappoint her. He wanted her to believe that he understood and loved her. She kissed him on the mouth, her eyes open.

Hunger

Who is Hanna? she asks.

They are sitting on the couch, watching the evening news.

Hanna?

Yes, Hanna. Who is she?

He doesn't respond.

There is a photo in your study of a woman, with dark, curly hair, 'Hanna' is written on the back, in your handwriting.

'Who is Hanna?' is a question she is asking today. Not fifteen years ago. Yet he cannot answer it.

A photo, you say?

I wouldn't ask if I didn't have an inclination as to

who she is to you. You slept with her, didn't you?

He doesn't respond.

He thinks she should be asking: 'Who is Younghee?' rather than 'Who is Hanna?'

You slept with her, didn't you? When was it? How long ago?

He doesn't respond.

They saw a marriage counsellor. For about two years.

They began by exploring their arguments. Both agreed they often turned violent, too violent. They were quick to explain the violence wasn't directed at each other. They did not hit one another. The counsellor asked them to describe what they considered as violent. Throwing plates and glasses on the floor – they laughed at how commonplace it sounded. Once, late at night, bottles of wine had been thrown from the house into the street. He stopped laughing when he remembered the incident; so did his wife. Anything else? the counsellor asked. He shrugged after glancing at his wife. Shouting? Strong words? Yes, of course. Aren't these violent too? His wife admitted they were. So did he.

He was not one to speak about his intimacy, particularly the lack of it; not one to speak about what made him unhappy, for he deplored being unhappy. He never talked about what was at the core of his unhappiness. Before they sat in the small room, on the two-seater simile leather couch facing Lissa, the marriage counsellor (didn't she call herself a 'therapist'?), he had not spoken about his marriage. He had not spoken to Edmonde about it. Not really; perhaps in superficial terms, when there was news to share, such as an upcoming trip to France with his wife, etc. He had never explained to his parents why they had decided not to have children. His marriage had been a great silence for those around him. Why had he not rupturted that silence; why had he not spoken to Edmonde about it?

With the counsellor, because his wife was sitting next to him, he never brought up his affairs. In the consultation room, he and his wife were in a kind of controlled environment where, at first, he thought he could bring anything up. But when he vaguely described how unfulfilled he had been, his wife often wept, and he thought it best not to get to the bottom of things for fear she would despair.

During one session he particularly upset his wife. He had prepared some talking points. He thought they would be helpful. He thought the analysis he had drafted that week on a park bench near his office, over two lunch breaks, would be helpful.

His wife had never become a mother, he declared to Lissa, and, by collateral address, to his wife sitting to his right. Why, since she had not become a mother, had she stopped being a lover? His case had been more detailed, with several layers of hypothesis, but that is how he now remembers it. Why had his wife, over time, stopped cultivating their intimacy? Because, clearly, she had. The consequence was that, in time, he had stopped regarding her as a lover. There had been no children to stand in the way of their love life, so why had it dissolved?

What a crude analysis, he thinks now with dismay. Then, he thought it some sort of breakthrough.

The affairs were very much on his mind when he was in Lissa's consulting room. Hanna. Had the affair with Hanna run its course when he and his wife saw Lissa every week? Had Hanna left? Often he wondered if Lissa could detect, when he spoke about his emotional state, that there was something else he hadn't mentioned that affected it. When he made eye contact with her – mostly when she spoke to him; he couldn't keep her gaze when he spoke – he sensed she knew about the affairs. Wasn't it obvious? Someone like him, considering the predicament he and his wife were in? But the affairs never came out; the names of Hanna, Younghee, others, were never pronounced. Had he wanted to do a thorough job of sorting his marriage out back then, the affairs might have been raised, and somehow put behind them.

He made an effort at home not to provoke his wife into arguments, and not to escalate those she started. He became quite good at it, so much so that his wife felt they no longer needed to see Lissa together. She suggested that perhaps he continue alone. The suggestion irritated him, but he thought he might then explore why, for instance, he'd stopped writing. Unlike his wife, he didn't feel the sessions with Lissa had turned their marriage around. They still seldom made love, but he was no longer bothered by that reality. He and his wife had in fact grown distant but there was peace at home.

His wife further suggested he discuss his parents with Lissa. In what way, he asked. You know, she said, you're not very communicative, your parents never really listened to you... You should talk about that with Lissa. The suggestion really got to him. He walked off without a word and went to the spare room.

During his sessions with Lissa alone, he talked a lot about writing. Most of his talking was about writing. The writing he had done in his youth, the writing he had not done since, the writing he wanted to do. He was loquacious, excited to talk about his early literary achievements. It felt good. He also spoke about his parents, exaggerating their supposed lack of listening and the history his wife had imagined, that of the boy growing up unheard.

He never mentioned Hanna to Lissa. He never mentioned his craving for sex with other women. He would have felt judged by her, even though he knew very well her position didn't allow her to judge him. But wouldn't she judge him on a personal level, have an opinion of him based on that confession of disloyalty? Lissa knew his wife. What stopped her from saying to her husband one evening, or to her friends over dinner: this patient of mine came with his wife for two years; now he comes alone, and guess what, he's just told me he's had an affair with some nymphomaniac… She and her husband would laugh, her friends would find her story priceless. She might even, on a personal level, be angry with him. He had noticed she and his wife often shared similar perspectives on what the three of them discussed; she would have, privately and silently, taken his wife's side. She would share with her husband and friends the contempt she had for that two-faced patient.

And that patient was him.

He and Hanna talked a lot. She did most of the talking.

She had travelled widely, with memories of distant places he knew he would never visit, and, in fact, had no wish to visit. He had not travelled much. In some of the places she had travelled, she'd become sick, and she told him about the illnesses. She told him of the long periods of convalescence when she returned home. When in Sydney she stayed with her parents. She wasn't married; she was alone. She was forty-something. He too was forty. No, he was in his mid-thirties. She looked like the woman he had almost married when he was in his early twenties. The woman he had almost married resembled the Breton woman named Gaud in Pierre Loti's novel *Iceland Fisherman*. So the woman he was talking to that evening at the party his wife had decided not to attend also looked like Gaud, the Breton woman. Her hair was black and thick and curly and not long.

They talked while others danced. They drank as they talked. They drank a lot. He saw she could drink a lot.

When the party was over and those who had danced were gone or sleeping on the floor, they left. He told her he could not invite her home because his wife was asleep there. She suggested they go to a hotel, and they found a plain chain hotel nearby.

She said, 'Looks like you need a little help…' and with her eyes locked on his, she slowly moved down to the end of the bed and took his soft penis into her mouth with her right hand. She looked up at him, at his face, his eyes, as she lubricated him with her saliva.

He said in a groan, 'I have drunk too much.' She

continued moving her head; then, smiling, she rose and rested her chin on his chest, looking up at him.

He wanted to say sorry.

They talked a lot that night. They talked about sex mostly. He had started it. She laughed and he laughed too. Then someone banged on the door and shouted, 'Will you shut the hell up!' They laughed again, more quietly this time, at the woman shouting from the door. He looked at the digital clock on the bedside table. It was five-twenty-something.

He would have to go home soon. His wife would be worried if she got up before he came back.

They kissed again. He moved above her and he managed to penetrate her with his half-erect penis. He moved languidly back and forth; his penis hardened slightly, but not much, it was still rather soft. He moved faster and very soon came. She did not.

He said, 'I should go.' She smiled at him. He got up to dress. It was now six-forty-something. Lying naked on top of the cover, she watched him. Dressed, he bent over to kiss her mouth. They kissed for a while, playing with each other's tongues; she sucked his. At some point he unbuttoned his fly, pulled down his trousers, and moved above her.

Her vagina felt immense, swallowing his penis, harder than before, yet still a little soft. Her vagina was so wet he could barely feel its walls. He thought of a misty, muggy swamp. He came quickly.

He gave the clock a quick glance before he left the room. It was seven-fifty-something.

When he got home, his wife was sitting on the couch in the living room. She was on the phone.

'Thanks, he's just got home. Sorry to have called you so early.'

Her face was red.

As he walked upstairs to shower and go to bed, he told her he had smoked marijuana and fallen asleep on the couch at the party.

§

At about the same time he met Hanna, as he was reading a book at a coffee shop a suburb away, he met Younghee. She too was reading. She was young, in her early twenties, he guessed. There was something European about her – the way she dressed perhaps – although her eyes were like those of a Japanese woman. He would discover later that her mother was Korean and her father Danish. But he could have met her in Paris, he thinks today, he could have met her when he was a student in philosophy. Could he really have met a young woman with a Korean mother and a Danish father back then in a city like Paris, he wonders. Not likely.

She was reading. She must read a lot, he thought.

As he got to know her, he realised that she read a lot. At her age he had only been reading for two or three years. She gave the impression of having read a lot, of having read *everything*. She had read a lot of books he had not read.

He interrupted her reading. He was sitting on the same long bench, a metre or so away from her. He had hesitated because he was reading a new Japanese author whose book he was not sure he would like. Correction: he liked his book and those that would follow but somehow was embarrassed to be seen reading them as they were easy and fast to read. He still preferred the classic Japanese writers but would read all of this new author's work with delectation.

He interrupted her reading by saying something banal to her, but then they quickly talked about the book she was reading.

It was by Knut Hamsun.

He had almost read Knut Hamsun. When he was in his late teens or early twenties. His friend then had read Knut Hamsun and encouraged him to read him. She had written about Hamsun's books in several of her letters to him. He remembers she had particularly enjoyed *La Faim*. Younghee was reading another book; she was reading *On Overgrown Paths*.

He lied: 'I haven't read *On Overgrown Paths*, but I have read *Hunger*...'

She smiled. 'I have too,' she said.

To avoid discussing *Hunger*, he said that Hamsun had tragically become a Nazi sympathiser during the 1930s. Another case of a writer of genius and despicable political views. She knew about this, seemed to know more than he. What she was reading dealt with this, she said. Was *On Overgrown Paths* an attempt to justify his views? he asked. No, she said, it was to say that he had not gone insane. And she told him about the book, which she had almost finished.

He now talked about Céline and the writer's political views, leading the conversation to French literature. And then he talked about Stendhal, whose oeuvre he had recently read entirely, and Stendhal's admiration for Napoleon Bonaparte.

It was a matter of time, he knew, and she did ask about the book lying under his hands and he had no choice but to tell her the truth – he was enjoying reading Haruki Murakami, even though he didn't think the book was very good.

She said nothing about Murakami, or whether one should enjoy a book that is not very good. He then thought that he most likely had said something she would not agree with. There was no shame in enjoying a book, even a book whose literary merits might not be as high as others one also enjoyed, she would rightly believe.

She asked him if he was a university lecturer. He was unsure whether it was a good thing or not that a young woman would take him for a lecturer. (He would not take a thirty-five-year-old, someone in their thirties, for a university lecturer, although there are lecturers in their thirties.) But then, he thought fleetingly, some young women do sleep with university professors, especially young women who read a lot.

He had not approached Younghee to, in time, sleep with her. He was compelled to talk to her by her allure and by her book. It would be later, as he got to know her, that the desire to sleep with her would grow and refuse to leave.

At the coffee shop they ended up talking a lot. She was finishing studies in anthropology. She had travelled considerably for someone her age. She went to live in Denmark for a year when she found out from her mother that her father was Danish. She never met or found her father.

Later, when she completed her studies, she left Australia, and she and he did not stay in touch. She was to travel a great deal, to take on a fascinating profession for which she would be known outside of her personal and professional circles. In magazines she would be called a 'global nomad'. She would go on to live in Japan, in India, in England, and in Finland by the time she reached thirty. She is now a world-renowned anthropologist working for a multinational technology company, an expert who figures what attributes mobile phones should possess to seduce consumers in the lower classes in India or the upper classes in Japan. He attended several of her public talks in Sydney. He sat in the audience, like hundreds of others, while she stood on the stage, alone or with a small panel, subject to everyone's gaze. He read a long profile of her in *The New Yorker* by the Annals of Technology staff writer.

§

When he made love with his wife or a mistress, he often thought, post-coitus, of books and stories. Those he did not write. Intense ideas sprouted in his mind there and then, and a whole book or story could have been written in those few seconds, had it been humanly possible. Then he lay down next to the woman and, for a handful of minutes, possessed the energy and courage to write the story. The story would unroll like a giant wave in a storm and his mind would ride it. And then he would fall asleep. He would not get up to fetch pen and paper. He would later wake to find the story murky and flawed, the enthusiasm dissipated, the prospect of what he would have to do to actually write it insurmountable.

Now he knows that, had he decided to isolate himself, say, Saturday mornings, Monday evenings perhaps, to 'open up the stories', as his aunt described that stage of the process, he would most likely have written several novels. Not many, and small ones, but the books would at least be there for him to see.

But on Saturday mornings he got out of bed and had breakfast with his wife while reading the newspapers or books written by others. While reading the papers and the books, he often thought about the past week's work and the office. He listened to his wife's plans for their next holiday, their next weekend away. Had he decided not to go away on weekends, he would have written a novel or two.

§

One morning during the week, a few days after their first meeting, he and Hanna met again at the hotel where they had slept together. She gave her name at reception and was told she wasn't welcome. Both surprised, in unison, they asked why. Guests had complained about the noise she and others had made in the room the night she had last stayed.

'Others?' Hanna said, as puzzled as he was. 'Which others? Only my friend and I stayed in the room. And yes, some irate woman banged on our door early in the morning, but I can't accept that we made a lot of noise. We talked, but not loudly. In fact, I would like to lodge a complaint about the woman who banged on our door like a demented person at five in the morning. I want to complain about the woman who complained about me.'

He saw that, as she said all this, Hanna was smiling.

'All right, all right,' the lone receptionist said. 'How many nights will you stay with us?'

'As few as we can,' Hanna replied, then turned to him. 'One night? One night until we can find another hotel?' Then, to the receptionist: 'Actually, just the day – we'll only stay until the evening.'

Hanna's parents were from another time and place, and she couldn't talk to them, she told him.

She talked to him a lot. She talked to him a lot about her work. She worked in Africa and liked it there. She was a doctor, and she liked black men, she told him. She spoke French, so sometimes they spoke French together. One evening he was talking on the phone to his aunt in Paris and Hanna asked him in French if she could suck his cock. He was unsure if he had understood and said yes, to avoid her having to repeat herself while his aunt was on the other end of the phone. So she unbuttoned his trousers and stroked his penis and when it got as hard as it could she put it in her mouth. He told his aunt he had to go and hung up.

She said she could not tell her parents her stories. She could not tell them she had lived in a *tukul* for a year in the south of the Sudan with only a goat for company and adulterated gin bought in a plastic bag from the local smugglers for her only alcoholic drink.

She told him how the governor of the province where she was based had wanted to sleep with her and kept requesting official meetings with her until the day he groped her. She ran out of his office. She had not known who to complain to; she had not known what to do. The governor might have sent people to kill her for fear that she would reveal the incident of the groping to her hierarchy, or worse to the Western press, and humiliate him. At that time, someone killed her goat and it was then she decided to come home for a while.

She told him of the naked men with muscly backs she had seen in all these war-torn countries. The naked black men who bathed in the Nile in the south of the Sudan.

She always fell ill upon her return home. She saw doctors, specialists in tropical diseases, but no one ever found the source of the symptoms.

She suffered from acute anxiety, she told him. She could not cope with shopping at a supermarket, eating at a restaurant, even a quiet one. She didn't sleep well unless she had drunk and made love most of the night. He remembered that, at the party where they met, she had sat away from the crowd and talked only to him all evening, once he had introduced himself. She had seen psychiatrists but no one seemed able to help.

He and Hanna drank a lot as they talked. That day at the hotel, he had brought rum, mint leaves and limes, and they drank mojitos. She decided which cocktail they drank and he bought the ingredients and brought the appropriate glasses.

§

Younghee told him she was haunted by a painter she had known in Copenhagen. Is he a real painter? He is an artist, she said. She showed him photographs of his drawings. He doesn't paint, does he? He draws; he's an artist who draws. He is an artist, she said.

He knew this Danish artist, who only drew, and whom she called a complete artist, was the one man she would remember. He told her so. She said he was wrong.

One evening over a drink at the Shakespeare's in Surry Hills, where they often met, she asked if he could get her a job, any job. She needed money to pay for her university courses, she explained. So he arranged a part-time, temporary job for her in the company where he worked.

Another time she told him about problems at his company, the bitchiness of female colleagues, and he burst into laughter. She fixed her gaze on him, perplexed, while he tried to stop laughing. Don't worry yourself, he said, it will pass. You're new at this, he said, I'm not, you should trust me.

After a long silence that evening, she told him the Danish artist had written: he was lost without her.

'Is that really what he wrote to you? That he is *lost without you*? That's senseless.'

'It's not. I see him in his studio: he can't do anything because I'm not there. He gazes at his drawings on the walls and he sees that they are nothing. Because I'm not there.'

'You left Denmark over a year ago…'

'It doesn't change the fact that I'm not there.'

'In my view it does,' he said before taking a sip of his drink.

He thought the Danish artist rather silly for a man of thirty-seven or thirty-eight. 'I'm lost without you,' he muttered, slowly shaking his head. 'Goodness!'

'Wasn't he lost *with* you? Didn't he look at his

walls when he didn't look at you, saying to himself that his drawings were nothing because when he looked at them he didn't look at you? Didn't he do anything then because you were there?'

Silence.

'Has he ever drawn you?'

'No.'

'Why?'

'He could not.'

'He obviously can't do much, your artist, can he? He's starting to annoy me.'

She exhaled smoke from her cigarette. He wished he had known what she was saying to herself.

§

At that time, the war in Chechnya was often on the news. He thought a lot about it. He read about Chechnya; he researched it. He had put together a 'map of the universe' of the Chechen conflict. Combatants at one extreme, the other, and those in between, and all the other actors: neighbouring countries, business people, military figures from each camp, and so on. He had also put together a list of issues and various implications. What was he going to do with this, he didn't know.

At that time, he was bored with his work and dreamt of achieving something important. How to achieve something of consequence? He racked his brain to find ways to transform his daydreams, his ideas, into actions. But how to go about it remained the eternal question on which he stumbled.

He didn't know how to go about it. He understood there was a multitude of things one could accomplish, choices of accomplishment – while others did these very things, he only thought of them. He knew that accomplishment required action, but he didn't know how to link the idea of accomplishing something with the action that would realise it.

In any case, at that time, unlike the Chechen rebels, if someone had asked him, What have you achieved?, he would have had to answer, I don't know, meaning *nothing*.

He and Younghee went to a literary festival to listen to a Russian journalist who is now dead. Murdered. She was to speak about Chechnya; she had written a book on the atrocities in Chechnya that he had read.

Younghee was wearing a thick red woollen jumper under a long leather coat. Smells of leather and tobacco as they embraced. In the hall of the theatre where the journalist was to speak, he saw some acquaintances. They did not know Younghee. They ought to have been surprised to see him in the company of a young woman, yet they smiled without innuendo as they said hello. They talked about this and that, as if he had been alone or with his wife. None of his acquaintances threw him a look that said, We thought you'd just got married, so what are you doing with this beautiful young woman with porcelain skin and black eyes? Worse still, they all looked at him and talked to him as if finding him in the company of a beautiful young woman had been natural, even expected.

The Russian journalist spoke in Russian; an interpreter translated what she said into English. The journalist spoke at length before the interpreter began translating into English. What the interpreter said in English was far shorter than what the journalist said in Russian.

He breathed in the leather and tobacco. He looked at Younghee – his friend – in the darkness of the theatre, from the corner of his eye. Her coat was on her lap.

There were Russians in the theatre speaking loudly among themselves; they ignored the interpreter, and those seated nearby prevented him and Younghee from hearing the translation. The journalist spoke of serious matters, but the Russians couldn't help talking among themselves. There were Russians his age, his parents' age, and even his grandparents' age. They spoke Russian among themselves.

He looked at Younghee and smiled. He would have liked to tell the Russians to be quiet – he would have, had he been alone or with his wife – but he said nothing. Would Younghee and he have talked too, had they been Russian? Perhaps. Somehow, the Russians seemed to have a right to talk during the conference – it was in Russian, after all, and about Russia and Chechnya.

The Russians talking in the audience grew in number and the sound of their voices in volume. There were no long loud whispers now, but conversations, full conversations, while the journalist was speaking.

He emitted a long, grave hush, which failed to quiet the audience but prompted the interpreter to demand silence.

A relative silence followed. And in that relative silence the journalist finished her address. A microphone was passed among the audience. Questions were asked and answered. We finished. We retrieved the microphone. But a Russian woman in the balcony still had a question. She asked to be allowed to ask it, he figured. The journalist and interpreter appeared not to have heard the woman and gathered their papers. The Russian woman grew excited and shouted something in Russian. He and Younghee watched the woman gesticulate and harangue the journalist as they left the theatre. They heard the journalist eventually say something to the woman, without the microphone.

In the theatre hall, Younghee's cheeks were red.

Your jumper is too thick, he said. She said she had no other. He knew she had bought it in Denmark.

§

He was thirty-three, wasn't he? Thirty-five, perhaps. He was a young man. Younghee was twenty-two. Hanna was thirty-eight or forty. His wife was thirty or thirty-one.

He was a young man but, to Younghee was he a young man? He was not. For a twenty-two-year-old woman, men of thirty-five are not young men, but men, with shallow yet perceptible crow's feet, sometimes rather deep, more pronounced. A thicker skin. The skin of the hands, or the torso or the neck toughened by the years. Like the Danish artist's skin, he presumes. That man was thirty-five when she met him. She was nineteen. Did she see him as a man the same age as the Danish artist? Or younger?

§

They had not known each other for long. His wife didn't yet know that he knew a young woman, a young Danish-Korean woman. He never talked about Younghee to his wife. Perhaps he would at some point. Perhaps later.

He didn't know what place to give Younghee. She was a friend. What would happen, where would the friendship lead, and when would it run its course, he didn't know. He was only beginning to form some desires as to what should follow.

§

They decided to go for drinks at the Shakespeare's after work.

She said, breaking a silence: 'We're working together.'

He was surprised. He could not remember suggesting anything which would drive her to say this.

After a few moments he thought: 'And so what, if we work together?'

Why is she saying this, as if he had made a proposal? The proposal, they both knew, even unsaid, existed. Hadn't she too made that proposal, considering the number of hours she had spent in his company? And considering the important – essential – things they talked about?

Did she say this to abort her own proposal rather than his? As if she had talked to herself, rather than to him?

They went on behaving as if no proposal had been made or as if it had been nipped in the bud.

His wife was on a business trip and he invited Younghee to come over for dinner. They did the grocery shopping together and dined together, face to face, at his place. There was a black-and-white photograph of his wife by the television.

'Is this your mother at your age?' she asked.

'My wife.'

'Oh.'

'I put her photo there when she's away,' he lied. The framed photo was always there.

Then he showed her another framed photo on the bookshelves of the spare room: one of Edmonde when she was his age. She looked at the aunt's photo for a while. He wished that she was saying to herself that his aunt was beautiful, or rather that there was something attractive about her, that she had made a positive judgment on her personality by looking at the photo.

He prepared dinner; she stood next to him, talking to him, sometimes looking over his shoulder to see what he was chopping. They were both drinking red wine. When the dinner was ready he sat at the dinner table, where his wife usually sat, and Younghee sat where he usually sat.

After dinner, he opened a bottle of the red wine Edmonde had given him when he was last in France. They had drunk two bottles of Australian red wine before he opened the French one. He had looked for a third Australian bottle but could not find one. The French bottle was of a very good wine and they would both enjoy it, he thought when he opened it. They could not stop drinking now so he had opened his best bottle. He had thought that once drunk they would dance to French folk music played with accordions, barefoot on the Persian rug of the living room, moving their arms in the air.

He was sitting on the couch. She too sat on the couch, turned towards him, sitting on her feet. She stretched and lay down, putting her legs on his lap. They talked. They talked about this and that as the *Hungarian Dances* accelerated. He should have changed the music, which was not propitious for talking but with her legs on him and the wine he had drunk, he didn't feel like moving.

They decided that she should stay with him. She would go back to her house when his wife came back from her business trip. A little before his wife came back. She would sleep on the day bed in the spare room. They would spend the next five days together. They would go to work together the days she worked.

The days she didn't work she would go out for walks, go to cafés with her friends or study. She would read in his living room, lying on the couch, or perhaps on the Persian rug, a cushion from the couch under her head or her stomach, if she lay on her stomach. She would read texts she was required to read for courses; she would write essays at the little table he sometimes used as a desk, in the spare room.

She would have the house key.

§

It would not be right to say he no longer appreciated his wife. He had not stopped appreciating her. Perhaps he appreciated her a little less because he had grown to appreciate Younghee (and, to a lesser extent, Hanna). But therein did not lie the problem. The problem was not whether he appreciated his friend more than he appreciated his wife. It was not a competition. The problem was: What would be the consequences on his marriage of his appreciation for Younghee, as it was clear that appreciating Younghee so much affected other compartments of his life, most of all, his marriage?

He decided not to discuss Younghee with Lissa and his wife at the marriage counselling sessions. While he didn't have an affair with Younghee, his wife, he knew, would think he *was* having an affair. An emotional affair.

He wrote to his aunt Edmonde the following letter about Younghee:

She has known one man. Next to her in the bed, the shape of his body, the hollow in the mattress. The hollow in the pillow. He is not with her; she no longer wishes him to be with her. Yet the hollow he has left remains.

This is where she is at. She would have liked to know other men. She would have liked to know other men instead of him, several instead of one. She now would like to know other men. She would like to know me. How, I do not know.

I look at her and I am starting to see her pain. I would like to talk to her about her face from different angles. I want to look at her. I look at her walk. Rolling a little. Gracious. I look at her eat. Roll her cigarettes.

I look at her hold her glass, I look at her exhale her cigarette's smoke. I listen to her. She reminds me of no one. She resembles no one I have known. I know her story. The love of my life, she refuses to call it, my madness, she calls it instead. What does youth make us say, make us do, make us believe? She is right to call her story this though. It is nothing else. Youth is right. One's life needs the love of one's life, and what follows.

And I? I, who would have liked to be the love of that life and who is not?

This man who is no longer there. This hollow in the mattress. In the pillow. Will always be there. The man won't count. She will no longer love him but she will dream about him. The man will be transformed into a story, her idea of the love of one's life. She doesn't know this yet and I will not be telling her. This man who made her think insane things, who rendered her insane, will make place for the idea of love. He will do no more to her. But I say nothing.

She will be with others and perhaps the hollow will never disappear. Not because of this man but because of youth and her young heart. Of youth's generosity. After this love of our life we become less giving, we become misers, without wanting to. We want to give everything but we are no longer able to.

There is still a hollow in my life. I do not call it my life's love, I call it pure loss. This 'love of our lives' is not complete but has the benefit of being blind.

This story that she told me and that I am telling you now is the story of the hollow in the mattress. Of the insanity of the first love. Of the discovery that one can forget oneself in another, in pain, in nothingness.

That is where she is at.

§

His wife was furious.

The evening she came back from her business trip, it was dark outside, she was squatting in front of the small wine cabinet and said, 'Where is the bottle you brought back from France? It's missing. Others are missing too.'

'It's not there?' he echoed.

'You drank it, did you? You drank it with her!'

She was now in front of him, staring him in the eyes. He was surprised and his face showed he was.

'Do you think I don't know she came here?'

Silence.

'You dined together! You think I wouldn't figure it out? The French wine was for you *and* me to drink.'

'But the Australian wine she and I haven't drunk is better; that's why I opened the Bordeaux…'

His wife's face was now red, tears ran down her red cheeks.

'Why did you open *this* bottle?' she cried. 'It was for you and me.'

'You exaggerate,' he said. 'Please calm down, we're only talking about a bottle of wine. There are other bottles left, and much better bottles.'

He now smiled at her.

She returned to the small wine cabinet, opened its little door and opened the front door of the house. From the small wine cabinet she seized a bottle from the bottom shelf, where the best wines were, and threw it in the street, against a tree. The bottle exploded and glass and wine scattered over the footpath. Then she threw another one. He walked up to the spare room. He heard several bottles explode against the tree and the footpath.

In the morning, his wife asked, 'Who is this woman with whom you drink our wine?'

'There is no woman,' he said, 'there's a girl who smells of leather and tobacco, as if she carried a leather tobacco pouch in her coat. She is a friend.'

§

Younghee told him that she was seeking new lodgings, in the suburb where he lived. She asked if this Saturday he wished to visit several houses with her. He said he would see.

Usually, on Saturday mornings he and his wife had breakfast together at a café nearby while they read the weekend papers or a book or the previous week's *New Yorker* magazine. They did not speak much.

He 'worked something out'. His wife had broken several bottles of wine earlier in the week, they had not spoken much all week so he told her that, this morning, he was going out alone.

Younghee was walking a little ahead of him. He thought about the muffled tread of a cat (she sometimes seemed to purr when she smoked). Younghee liked silence. But during her silences, she sometimes purred. Like a cat.

Soon after she found a room in a boarding house two or three blocks from where he lived, Younghee told him that she was moving back to Denmark. He was speechless, and she too fell silent after having told him. They drank their beers, then played a game of darts, then drank more beer and talked about work. When they parted, she said, 'Will you write to me?'

The following week he brought to their last meeting at the Shakespeare's a postcard from his collection. It was of a painting by William Young, *The Musician*, from the Art Gallery of South Australia. The musician in a tuxedo rests his right arm on the piano. His left elbow on his left thigh, his right hand supports the right side of his face. His small black eyes, anyone can see it, are sad. The musician looks out into the room; he doesn't look at anything specific.

He said to Younghee, 'The musician has lost his singer. Her voice resonates in his head. He has done nothing with his life, he seems to think, and now that he has lost his songstress he is crushed by that fact, that he has done nothing with his life. It was fine to have done nothing with his life as long as she was singing to the music he played…'

He now read the inscription in the painting: 'Sunt Lachrymae Rerum, his leaf has perished in the green, in narrow ways his life has run, the world which credits what is done is cold to all that might have been.'

'It's from a poem by Alfred Tennyson,' she said. 'The second line is wrong though, it should be *And, while we breathe beneath the sun…*' Then she added, after a short silence, that this poem and the sad little black eyes of the musician in the tuxedo lost in the nothingness of the music-bar should not augur for him the emptiness he thought would come with her departure.

He had thought she would see the Danish artist in the musician but it was himself that she saw.

'I think I am suffering,' he said. 'You make me suffer.'

She smoked a lot. She was smoking. She exhaled smoke from her mouth. He thought that she must have found his suffering benign compared to the suffering she and the Danish artist had known and still knew.

A few years earlier, he had read an unimportant short novel by a Japanese writer. An immigration officer befriends a voice – a 'distant voice'. Not a ghost but a woman's voice, a woman who seems to exist, to be a person somewhere in Tokyo. The immigration officer never sees her, only hears her voice when he is in his apartment. She tells him things about herself. This voice turns his life upside down. Notably, it convinces him, somehow, to not get engaged to his girlfriend; and because he cannot think of anything else but the woman's mysterious existence and what the voice says to him, he is unable to perform the functions of his immigration job satisfactorily. The voice becomes the most important element of his life. It drives him away from what is not essential and from what has, in appearance, made him happy, like the engagement to his girlfriend.

Would his friend Younghee become a distant voice? A voice he could not ignore? He could not push the person away. Would he be able to push the voice away? In any case, it seemed to him that it would have been easier to explain the existence of a voice to Lissa and to his wife than to explain Younghee. It would have been easier to come across as insane.

§

Out of the blue, he stopped by a chain bookstore near his office to find *Hunger* by Knut Hamsun. It is not in stock, he was told by an attendant, but since it exists it can be ordered. He said to the attendant, no, thank you.

He walked to the small French bookstore at the edge of the Central Business District. The owner greeted him in his usual warm manner, with a strong handshake and a loud *comment ça va* in what always appeared to be a tone of surprise, and rushed to the back of the shop to brew two cups of coffee. When Claude, for that was the name of the shop's owner, returned from the back shop and they were done with the small talk, he asked if he held a copy of Knut Hamsun's *La Faim*. Claude looked at him over his semi-circle reading spectacles with a smile, in which one could read a kind of philosophical disappointment, and exclaimed *bien sûr!*

It was an old edition of the Presses Universitaires de France, but in very good condition. It was not cheap but it was a nice book and to him it did not matter if books were expensive. He said he would take it and Claude slid it in a paper bag. He stayed a little longer after having paid to talk about the Sydney weather, French politics and the incompetent staff of the Embassy and the Alliance Française. They laughed at how the French community in Sydney resembled the small and pathetic bourgeoisie of Yonville surrounding Emma Bovary and how the Ambassador looked like a mouse, wearing a suit too big for his skinny little body – so much for the *rayonnement de la France!* Claude said clutching his ribs.

Claude, he knew, was a recluse who did not mingle with the French of Sydney although he was the most polite of hosts when someone, French or not, visited his bookshop. But Claude despised the social vectors at work in groups and 'layers of society'. He understood Claude and sometimes thought he was a little like him, a little misanthropic.

On the bus home, he started reading *La Faim*. His wife was home when he got there. He told her he had to read this book and that she should not wait for him for dinner, she should go ahead and leave him alone. She said fine while continuing what she was doing when he had come in, as if she had half-heard him. He went to the spare room and read the book, lying on the day bed, until he finished it. Then, out of exhaustion, like Hamsun's narrator on many occasions, he cried.

Just before dawn he thought of presenting himself crying to his sleeping wife but quickly decided against it. She had not read the book. She had never written a story or an essay and didn't know what writing was. She had never cried while reading a book. She was alien to creative hunger, devoid of creative demons. He stayed in the spare room pondering whether that day he would go to work or not.

Something akin to the hunger Hamsun's character suffered had prevented him from writing. It was not poverty. He was unsure as to whether Hamsun's character should have been seen as a genius, struggling with his living conditions or a fool not coping with his living conditions, handicapped by his foolishness and laziness. Hamsun's character starts an essay and then some thought drags him away and he starts writing a play and doesn't finish the essay, and never completes the play. His landlady doesn't believe him when he says he will sell some of his writing and pay the rent. He cannot write, nor can he not write. He had not had that problem when he wrote, he had almost always been able to focus on a piece of writing until completion. So why had he stopped writing? And why was he not writing again? Had the landlady in him been convinced all along that he would not be able to pay the rent with his writing?

He was going to talk to his wife all those years ago. I need to write, you see. I have not written in years and it is now that I need to stop what I am doing, perhaps for three or six months, and write. She would have said, of course, I will support you in this, or whatever you wish to do. He would have then gone to the office and requested special leave for six months. He did not.

Albert Cohen dictated his texts to his wife and, in doing so, he improvised and added to the story as he went; Cohen did not write but spoke his novels. He would have not worked that way. With two fingers, the index fingers of each hand, he would have slowly typed on the keyboard of his computer. This slow typing would have suited him since sentences would have come to him slowly. And if sentences had come faster, though never at great speed, he would have controlled their flow. And when a lot had to be written, he would have ingested the ideas, the paragraphs like a boa constrictor swallowing a large prey to then digest them on the keyboard at the rhythm of the two fingers.

He would have rarely added to the sentences or paragraphs punctuated at their end by the flashing cursor on the screen. Rather he would have deleted. He would have deleted a lot. Most of the time nothing would have remained and he would have had to abandon writing for the benefit of another activity that would have seemed less derisory and inutile. Like watching television.

He would have turned the spare room into his study and in the morning in his study, he would have turned his computer on and prepared a file. Then, at his desk he would have read every single page of *Le Monde* and *Le Figaro* from the previous week. He would have looked through books on his shelves for inspiration. He would have made a few notes on index cards to be used later, when typing his text.

He would have made himself lunch at lunch time or gone to one of the neighbourhood cafés for a sandwich and a coffee.

In the afternoon, with a cup of Lapsang Souchong tea on the coffee table, legs stretched out onto the footrest in front of the couch, satisfied with the notes made on the index cards and inspired by books he had leafed through, he would have watched *Letters and Numbers* on television. He was on average not as good as the contestants on the show, whether it be for the letters or the numbers conundrums, but he was not far from their levels either. He preferred the numbers. He struggled to find words of more than six letters when the letters were displayed.

Then in his study, he would have gone back and forth between the books on the shelves, the index cards and the computer. Soon there would only have been an hour or two before his wife would get home and therefore not enough time to get further into anything, or get into anything at all, to read or write. So he would have sat in front of the television with another cup of tea. When his wife would get home in the evening, he would have just finished watching the French quiz show *Questions pour un champion* on cable.

Or he would have found in a box under the day bed in his study the photocopied manuscript of *Argol* by Julien Gracq. He would have had the first few pages framed and hung on a wall in his study. Then he would have been ready to start. He would have looked at the hand-written words in Gracq's neat manuscript then bent over his notebook to write his. His computer would have been in the cupboard and he would have written with a ballpoint pen, like when he had started writing. He would have written more and better than he had ever had.

He would have sat at his desk, gazing out the window or looking at *Argol*'s manuscript on the wall. He would have written several small paragraphs, almost a page. A shiver of self-satisfaction would have run along his spine. Not so fast, he would then have thought, briefly. Still he would have savoured this moment of feeling heroic a little longer. Others will never write like this, he would have said to himself. What a piece of writing! It's very good, well written. He would have had no complaint about what he had written. If only a whole book could be done like this, then it would be done.

The following day, after rereading these paragraphs, he would have laid down on the bed in his study, not far from the computer with the previous day's writing on the screen. The previous day's writing would still be very good. Barely a page now, after corrections, but what a page! He would have laid down, as he often did, to wait. He would have waited like one waits for the phone to ring. He would have waited for *it* to come. For the rest. For what follows. For the words to come down from who knows where in his brain and flow onto the white page. What would have come that day would mostly have to do with waiting for words, words about waiting for words. Words which reflected themselves like objects between two mirrors facing each other.

There would have been no guarantee that the day after that day, and the following days would have been any different. He would have written a good page in a week, or two weeks, or three weeks. And then what, how long could he have spent lying down and waiting?

In any case, his wife wouldn't have asked, 'Did you work well today?'

He therefore didn't have to respond, 'Not really. I wrote letters this morning. I sent old short stories in French to two magazines, one in Sydney, one in Perth…'

And she wouldn't have to follow with: 'You don't need not to work to send old French stories to Australian magazines. You need to write now.'

And he: 'Writing letters is writing…'

'Writing to your friend in Denmark or God knows where is not writing a novel,' she didn't have to end up saying.

She didn't have to say that stopping work and not writing, or writing a little, and writing to his friend, and doing practically nothing else was a betrayal, to himself and to her.

Week after week, he would have seldom written and would have not perceptibly improved at *Letters and Numbers* and *Questions pour un champion*, at least not enough to be a contestant on the shows.

It would have been with gratitude to his wife for not starting this conversation that one evening he would have announced that he had decided to get back to the office.

He lacked what his wife never lacked, it strikes him today: obstinacy. Without it he could not be other than what he has been. He could not live the dream that inhabited his younger self, nor fulfil the ambition he wished he had nurtured and worked for since he finished his studies and had to take a job. Writing had been his past, was a few years of his life, his youth, it is a few stories and a few essays on art. He took a plane like Hamsun's narrator took a ship, like Hamsun himself, but unlike Hamsun or his character he has not come back with writing.

Has he been dejected all along? No he has not. He has not tried much to write and he has not grieved much over the short stories that once existed, until now. But that morning years ago after reading *La*

Faim, he felt the acute prick of regret. And on such occasions his regrets spread over all the other aspects of his life.

He would write to Younghee. But could he tell her about his reading of *La Faim* – wasn't he supposed to have read it fifteen years ago? He could have said that he had reread it but how could one be moved to that point again, at a second reading? How to deal with this imperious need inhabiting him today to share his emotions about the reading and the subsequent thoughts? Younghee would have thought him sentimental if he had been moved as he was at the second reading, what's more, in his mid-thirties. And what would she have thought of him for not having pursued writing when he was in his twenties?

§

Hanna had decided that they should drink martinis, gin martinis, so he brought two bottles of gin and a bottle of vermouth, two martini glasses and a cocktail shaker. He also brought three bottles of white wine. Tonight they were to stay at a hotel a short stroll away from the Sydney Opera House. His wife was on a work trip and he and Hanna were to spend two days and two nights together. He had called work to say he was unwell and unable to come to the office.

He had arrived first and paid for the room. The small room had a plunging view over the Botanic Garden from its main window. The sun was setting and the bats from the garden had started their evening migration to Centennial Park, or wherever they spent their nights. He drew the curtains, turned off the main light and turned on the small lights.

Hanna was wearing a short, black evening dress and earrings, and her face was lightly made-up. Her hair seemed to also have more volume than usual. She told him she had been to the beautician and thought she should dress well tonight. She was chewing gum.

Hanna entered the room and did not look about it, she embraced him and kissed him. She quickly unzipped and unbuttoned his trousers and pulled them down and put his penis in her mouth. He was standing. His penis erect in her mouth. He saw the reflection of her, kneeling, on the screen of the black television set. He saw her bottom almost showing as the short dress was lifted up, he saw her legs crossed at her ankles and her red high heels and he saw her curly hair move. For a second he thought of the gum she was chewing when she came into the room.

Then they kissed again and she pushed him onto the bed and sat on him, seizing his penis and introducing it into her. Her vagina was very wet and seemed to spurt liquid now and then. Her dress was down around her stomach and his hands were on her bare breasts. Quickly he came inside her.

She asked if they could start with wine. He opened a bottle and on the bed they talked about this and that. He described the 'clouds of bats' he had seen flying out of the Botanic Garden when he had arrived. She talked about her parents' latest racist remarks about her brother's girlfriend, who was of Chinese descent.

They finished the bottle. She unbuttoned his shirt and kissed his chest and then moved her tongue around his nipples, she gently bit them. His nipples and his penis became hard quickly and he pushed her aside and turned her over so he could penetrate her from behind. Now he saw her face reflected in the black television screen, and her breasts swaying back and forth. He came quickly.

Her dress was crumpled at the waist and she took it off. He lay down on the bed and she too lay down, alongside him, her head at his toes. She took the almost empty bottle of white wine and drank the few drops left in it and pushed its neck into her vagina. She moved the bottle in and out; her groans grew louder. He saw her hands on the bottle. Her eyes were closed. He felt his penis stiffen again, which surprised him. He grabbed it rather strongly with his right hand and started masturbating, looking at her face. He wanted to bring his penis to her mouth but did not. He kept masturbating while she was moving the neck of the bottle inside herself.

She opened her eyes and dropped the bottle on the carpeted floor. She sat up and watched him masturbate for a while. He felt he had no semen left in him and that no matter how long he masturbated nothing would come out. He went to her and lay on her and easily entered her. Again, his softly erect penis was lost in the wetness. But he moved slowly inside her, and soon came again, softly and briefly.

They stayed in bed for the two days and nights. They talked a lot. Between sex. She told him about Sierra Leone, The Congo, Liberia, Nigeria, The Sudan and Guinea. He could not imagine what these places looked like. He could not imagine how she lived and what her work consisted of. He told her this repeatedly as she related her stories. She told him about Charles Taylor and the evil he had committed and what it meant to the people she had met there. He had heard the name of Charles Taylor on the news.

She told him how in her late twenties she had had a 'bad phase'. She lived in France then, she was between assignments. She took, bought and sold drugs, mostly cocaine. He was surprised. Why, he asked. I don't know, she responded. Probably because of the people I hung around, because of my boyfriend.

'Who was your boyfriend?'

'Nobody, really.'

'Was he dealing drugs? Was he a drug-dealer?'

'He was a waiter in a café. That's how we met. I had a coffee where he worked. He did drugs. But not a lot. Some of his friends were full-time dealers,' she said.

As they talked they kept drinking. He had made good martinis at first but now they were sloppy. He no longer shook them in the cocktail shaker and he no longer added lemon zest or peel. He simply poured a little vermouth from the bottle standing on the bedside table then gin from the blue bottle next to the vermouth. On occasion Hanna took gulps of gin from the bottle. The gin was no longer cool.

As they talked they sometimes fondled each other. He had also brought books from which he read her passages.

He had stopped counting the number of times he had come. His ejaculations on the second day consisted of a few drops and he found it more and more difficult for his penis to become even the slightest bit erect, although late in the morning after the first night, when he had woken up, he had been very excited and could not lose his hard-on no matter how many times he came.

Her boyfriend from Paris, she said, was tall and very handsome. He was from The Congo. She took drugs with his friends, who were also from The Congo. Too many drugs, she let out a big sigh.

He told her how at twenty, studying philosophy in Paris – perhaps we passed each other in the street, he interjected – he fell into a depression. He fancied himself as a writer, he wanted to become a writer, and depression, he first thought, would be the perfect condition to be in to write. That was not so, he found out. He could not write. For that matter, he could barely read. It was truly depressing, he said jokingly. He took no drugs because he did not know where to find them and he was afraid of the places where you could find them and of the people who offered them. He probably could have not afforded to buy drugs anyway. So for a while he had stayed home. He remembered spending two weeks in bed, only getting up when he could no longer hold his bladder or his bowels had to move. He watched his little television but could barely see it from his bed so he really only half-watched television, he listened to it. He continuously listened to one or two tapes of music. He barely ate and didn't wash. He stank. His studio apartment stank. No one called, except his parents, but he let the answering machine record their messages. He slept a lot but his sleep was not a restful one, in fact he felt like an insomniac. His dreams were of the same stuff as his thoughts when he was awake. He was exhausted no matter how much he slept.

Then someone from university he barely knew

called him and left a message on his answering machine, inviting him to a party at a nightclub. Two days after the message, the day of the party, hungry and exhausted, he called back his acquaintance and said yes, he'd like to come, thank you.

He got up early in the afternoon and felt it was a bad idea and went back to bed. He slept until the evening. He got up and again thought it was a bad idea but damn it, he could not spend his life in bed, he said to himself. Then as he was standing naked, and cold, in his tiny bathroom about to jump in the shower, his penis rose.

As he was telling the story his penis rose and Hanna grasped it gently with her right hand, moving her hand up and down slowly, like a caress.

His penis rose, he said, but he could not find the strength to masturbate. He felt no desire. No image, no memory came to mind. While showering the erection subsided. He washed his hair several times and scrubbed his beard with shampoo. He scrubbed his skin with a nail-brush. He was truly dirty, he said, he felt very dirty. He washed his genitals several times too, his pubic hair with shampoo after the soap. It was hard work, he said, because he was exhausted and in reality he did not want to wash. Washing himself felt unexplainably harmful.

He combed his long hair. He remembered thinking, when did it grow? Looking in the mirror, he saw small crevasses on his nose. No, big crevasses, and again he felt he should stay home rather than showing the crevasses to people at a party.

In front of the tall and narrow wardrobe, he wondered what he should wear. Then the question became what he could wear for he only owned a few trousers and T-shirts and sweat-shirts and all were dirty.

It was spring, he remembered, so he put on a T-shirt and on top, an orange short-sleeve shirt.

The ends of his white T-shirt shown from under the sleeves of his shirt. Was he wearing jeans? Most likely.

It was still light outside when he left his apartment. It is a bad idea, he thought, as he turned the key to lock his door. Outside there was a light, warm breeze and his hair moved a bit in it and to his surprise it felt good.

He walked to the station and took the suburban train. In the train a few people read and he wished he had brought a book.

He felt okay, not too anxious, though he missed his bed. He felt that now, if he were in bed, he would read, but he stayed on the train and waited for his acquaintance outside of the nightclub when he got there. As he waited sitting on a step of an open porte cochère a couple of doors from the club, he thought it was a truly pleasant Parisian spring night. He felt okay.

All changed when with his acquaintance and his acquaintance's friends and he entered the nightclub. It was overcrowded and the deafening, unlistenable music seemed to have made people mad. Those on the dance floor were in a kind of trance. He wanted to leave straight away. There was no train home though, it was too late, and the first morning train would depart in a few hours. A walk in the streets of Paris at night would beat staying in the nightclub, he was sure of that.

Before leaving he went to the bar. He had not drunk for over two weeks. He looked at the bar menu and counted he could probably afford three drinks, two whiskies and a beer. So he ordered a whiskey, with a couple of ice-cubes.

He had turned his back to the dance floor and by now, the music did not matter to him, it no longer travelled to his brain. Someone said to him, someone on his right, 'You have a beautiful face.'

He turned to the person, the young woman who had said these words. *She* had a beautiful face. She was looking at him, in the eyes, so there was no confusion – *she* had said this to him.

He felt like saying that it was dark, how could she see his face, but said nothing. He had not spoken in two weeks, save the few words on the phone to his acquaintance, accepting the party invitation.

He turned back to his drink, still facing the bar, and she came closer. She also turned her back to the dance floor. Her bare left arm touched his right arm. In fact they were touching for the whole length of their forearms. How strange and pleasant it was to have his skin in contact with someone else's skin. Her skin was soft, he thought, but any young woman's skin would be soft. He turned his face to her and smiled.

'I am a photographer,' she said 'and I would love to photograph your face.'

‘People your age, my age, are nothing, they’re students at best. You’re a photographer as much as I am a writer.’

‘I make a living out of photographing people and things,’ she said. ‘I have never studied. I really want to photograph you.’

He started to look more closely at her face, rather than turning his away to stare at the bottles on the wall behind the bar. She was truly beautiful and her facial skin seemed the softest. He thought of inviting her to dance, but he could never imagine himself dancing.

‘Do you drink a lot?’ she asked.

He smiled and said that he could not afford to drink *a lot*.

She asked if he danced and he said no.

She invited him to go to the dance floor. For a few minutes only, she promised. He said okay.

He could barely move his body, which was

exhausted, but he was now light-headed thanks to the whiskey and he took her hands in his and danced, moved, as well as he could.

She must have felt his fatigue, or felt bored of dancing with someone who moved like a wooden, string puppet, or felt that she had fulfilled her promise to dance a few minutes only, for she led him back to the bar after a short moment. They talked. Then another young woman, of equal beauty, burst in between the two of them.

'And who is this charming young man?'

He felt irritated at the word 'charming'. He could not fathom how he had a *beautiful face* and now was *charming*. He thought this was the typical hypocritical way wealthy young Parisians addressed each other, with flattery.

He swore to himself.

The young woman who had just positioned herself between him and the other young woman introduced herself as Sofia. She had a Maghrebi accent. She bought a round of whiskey for the three of them. She and the other young woman, whose hair was of a brilliant red, talked for a while. He figured they knew each other. Then they started arguing. And he figured it was because of him, which amused and concerned him at the same time. He said to them, nice meeting you and thanks for the drinks but it is time I go home now.

He had walked out of the nightclub when he realised that the two young women were following him. Let us invite you for a drink, said the young red-haired woman, who had said her name was Hélène. At my place, I live a block away, she said.

As he walked into the apartment with one large room, he deduced the two young women lived together and shared the same bed. And he was right for they soon sat on their bed in the main room with drinks, and kissed like a couple who still had tenderness for one another. He looked elsewhere. There were framed photos of landscapes and people on the walls, mostly black and white. He thought nothing of them.

The light in the apartment was not strong but brighter than in the club and he thought of the crevasses on his nose and stood up to say good-bye.

They whispered to each other and Hélène said, 'Stay with us tonight.'

'Okay,' he said. He did not ponder the proposal because he didn't have the energy, he explained to Hanna. He knew he didn't have the energy to roam the streets until the first train so he had said okay. He looked at Sofia who gave him a smile he took as her confirmation of the consensual nature of the offer to stay.

He sat down again on the two-seater couch and sipped his whiskey. Hélène went to him and sat on his lap, and kissed him softly. His penis became as hard as a rock in an instant and it somehow hurt him. The kiss became more intense. Then he felt a pair of hands moving on his lap. Hélène's hands were on his face, on his cheeks, or on the nape of his neck or in his hair. Hélène moved to sit next to him and Sofia who was kneeling between his legs moved up and sat on his right thigh. She was now kissing him and her kiss was wet and she moved her tongue over his lips and in his mouth. So he started moving his tongue too.

He told Hanna that he had wanted to make love to Hélène more than to Sofia. They were both of equal beauty but his body yearned more for Hélène's so when he kissed or fucked Sofia, it was to get it over with and be with Hélène.

At some point, Sofia tried to kiss Hélène but Hélène turned away from her and kissed him. Sofia tried to kiss him but he kept going back to Hélène after quickly kissing Sofia.

He slept next to Hélène on the far right side of the bed. Hélène had slept in the middle.

Hanna was listening to him intently lying on her stomach, over the bed cover, still holding his half-erect penis. He stopped telling his story for a while, he could not see the point of taking it further. As he was silent Hanna moved her hand with a little more intensity, looking vacantly at his bare chest.

A few hours after he had stopped his story about Sofia and Hélène, Hanna said she wanted to tell him a sex story too. He didn't think he could make love to her again today or drink one more drop of alcohol so he was happy to listen to her and then sleep. She started her story:

Her boyfriend's name was Mamadou, and, as she had said, he was a tall and handsome man. She would sit in his small and basic apartment most of the day and take drugs. At night, when he came home, they would fuck. Most of the night. Mamadou was insatiable, she said, and she was drugged out of her mind. The only thing she never allowed, even when out of her mind, was to be sodomized. She didn't understand how some women like being sodomized. I told Mamadou, she said, don't go there.

One day Mamadou had a friend staying with him. Some guy who had just arrived from The Congo. As tall and handsome as Mamadou. After a few days he asked Mamadou if he could fuck her. Mamadou said yes. She didn't mind. So they fucked and Mamadou was there looking at her pussy and his friend's cock moving in and out of it. It was nice. Then Mamadou fucked her. They proposed that one fucked her in the ass and the other her pussy, at the same time, but she said, Mamadou, remember what I said about that and they dropped the idea. For two or three days they fucked like this, Mamadou's friend then Mamadou and so on. In the morning, they would run a bath for her and the two of them would wash her gently. I felt like a queen, she said.

She stopped the story and played with his right nipple. He said nothing but started feeling hot and his stomach started churning. They fell asleep and when he woke up several hours later he still felt nauseous.

He read her the beginning of 'From a Bush Log Book 1', a story from Frank Moorhouse's book *Forty Seventeen*. The protagonist and his mistress, Belle, who are on a trip along the coast, 'had debauched in motel room and restaurants' and Moorhouse describes their bed sheets as 'drenched with champagne and with all the smells and fluids that two bodies could be made offer up in such dark love-making…'

He remarked that champagne had not been spilled onto their sheets while every other possible alcohol had and he called room service to order a bottle. It would be for their breakfast.

With the champagne they kissed and slowly they started making love, he on top of her, lying on the bed. She lifted her legs, as she had always done when in this position, and rested them on his shoulder. His mind was rather blank, too tired to process the fact that it was likely the last time they made love. He was deep inside her.

The two days and nights had passed and they needed to go home. His penis was inflamed and when he returned home he had to hide it from his wife for several days, by wearing pyjamas in bed. Soon Hanna was to fly off again to Africa. He had left with her the books he had brought. She should take them with her to Africa, he had said. In the street, outside the hotel they embraced. She walked away. He stood there for a while. He looked out in her direction to see if she would turn back. In any case, her eyesight was not good and from where she was, should she had turned back, she would not have seen him clearly.

Voyage à Carcassonne

Artists are by no means men of great passion but they often *pretend* to be, in the unconscious feeling that their painted passions will seem more believable if their own life speaks for their experience in this field. [...] But deep-rooted passion, passion which gnaws at the individual and often consumes him, is a thing of consequence: he who experiences such passion certainly does not describe it in dramas, music or novels.

Nietzsche. *Human, All Too Human* 211

He was a precocious young man. That is how he sees his seventeen-year-old self today. With a smile at the naivety of the thought, he sometimes tells himself that he achieved then what he still wants to achieve now. He wanted to be a writer, and what he wrote then was good. The smile vanishes. He has not written in a long time; he stopped writing in his early twenties when he got a job, then a career. There is no novel. There is no longer any short story. There has not been a short story for thirty-six years. That is what has sometimes troubled him when, in the night, he has woken and work matters have not assailed his somnolent mind, that there was no writing. There have been some ideas quickly put down with various pens and pencils on index cards. Brilliant ideas sometimes, possibly seeds for great literature. At thirty-three, he remembers saying to himself that thirty-three was Jesus's age; at thirty-five, that thirty-five was Mozart's age; at thirty-eight that Céline had published *Journey to the End of the Night* at thirty-eight… If he looked carefully through his files, he would find index cards recording these thoughts about age and accomplishment. He is fifty-something, and he has not written *Journey to the End of the Night*. He has pursued as best as he could a career he did not anticipate. With a career like his, it would not have mattered if he had died at thirty-three or thirty-five. With a career like his, one's achievement is to complete it and retire a little earlier than the standard retirement age.

He keeps his writing – the stories published in small literary magazines and university journals, drafts, etc. – and the letters he received as a young man and a thin black box in the bottom drawer of his desk in the study. He goes back to them now and then.

He knows very well the contents of the black box but often he is drawn to open it and inspect the little things inside. Each time he opens the box and holds these small things in his hands, they appear new to him, and he spends some time rediscovering them.

There is a page detached from a small notebook, folded in half. On the page, he recognises his handwriting. The handwriting he had then. He had written two telephone numbers. One is probably hers. Then, below, an itinerary. It reads:

Bus at 7.10
Arrives in Toulon at 7.50

Then 8.27 train
Arrives in Marseille at 9.08

Leaves Marseille at 9.20
Arrives in Montpellier at 10.55

———

Train leaves Montpellier at 14.59 (the '59' was corrected; he had written '53', it seems to him, then changed the '3' to '9'. He remembers his eyesight was not good then and he didn't wear glasses.)
Arrives in Toulon at 17.19

Bus leaves Toulon at 17.55
Arrives in Bormes-les-Mimosas at 18.35

Little train at 19.00.

Yes, he took the little train to get from the small holiday house his parents rented to the shops or to the bus station. The little train was free and carried holiday-makers around the small town of Bormes-les-Mimosas.

In the black box, there are also two Société Nationale des Chemins de Fer train timetables: *Bordeaux – Nice* and *Nice – Bordeaux* for 2 June

1991 to 28 September 1991. And the bus table from the Société Départementale des Transports du Var with summer schedules on one side for *Toulon – Le Lavandou – St Tropez* and on the other for *St Raphael – St Tropez*, for 7 July 1991 to 9 September 1991.

He has kept the train, bus, and Bormes-les-Mimosa's little-train tickets. From going through the train tickets, he sees again that he visited Montpellier twice in a week. There are a number of bus tickets to Palavas, which they reached by bus from Montpellier to go to the beach during that time together.

On the back of the page with the itinerary, her address is written in her handwriting. She had specified 'Care of Mr Voyat'. He remembers her place, and he remembers the name of her lodger. Yes, it was Mr Voyat.

There is a hair clip, an empty perfume sample that has completely lost its fragrance, and a passport photo of her dated on the back 'February 1991', again in her handwriting, her first name and 'February 1991'.

After the summer holidays of 1991 they wrote to each other. He has kept her letters, she has his. Unless she destroyed them. He cannot read what he wrote to her. He didn't make copies of his letters. What did he write to her? Did he tell lies in his letters? He knows he did.

They sent books to each other and tapes with music. On the back of the front cover of Brecht's *Baal*, which she had sent him, it said 'someone who loves you…' She had written this. The only time or place she had said this to him. She was often more cryptic about her feelings towards him. Or about anything. In her ink and handwriting the sentence didn't mean the same as when his girlfriend from high school had confessed to loving him.

§

In Carcassonne lived an artist he was to interview. At seventeen, he had started studying philosophy at one of the capital's universities, and to earn pocket money he wrote texts about painting for leaflets for commercial art galleries. He had once been asked to write two thousand words or so for a catalogue. The pay had been good, and he'd been sent to spend a weekend with the painter at his castle near Bordeaux. The artist he was to meet in Carcassonne had the name of a musical instrument: Guitard. The funny thing, he was to discover, was that Jean-Louis Guitard did play the guitar. With such a name, Guitard had felt compelled to learn the instrument. He had figured that, with such a name, he would often be asked whether he played the guitar and whether he could play it there and then, so when he was eight he decided to learn to play the guitar.

The year after his trips to Montpellier, he told his friend in a letter that he would be in Carcassonne in June and asked whether she might meet him there, if Carcassonne wasn't too hard to reach by train and she was free that weekend. She had no plans and would have dropped them, had she had any, to meet him in Carcassonne, she had replied. He was elated.

He finds her response about the Carcassonne trip in a letter from March that year. He reads her response to the Carcassonne proposal again. He had been thrilled when he first read her letter. He now wonders what had pleased him more – that they would see each other in Carcassonne, or that she would cancel plans to see him. She for him.

Why does he still think about those days? Why, from time to time, perhaps once or twice a year now, does he open the thin black box and reminisce about Montpellier and Carcassonne?

He barely remembers Carcassonne, the city itself. He sees in his mind the well-known image from school history books or postcards of the city's fortified walls. He remembers a bench by a river with a small park around it, but he isn't certain that the bench and park of his memories were those of Carcassonne, or of somewhere else. He remembers that, at the time, he thought the small park dirty. Was it the park in Carcassonne or somewhere else? He has sat in many small parks since then. Why can't he remember what precisely made him think the park was dirty? He doesn't know whether there were plastic bottles, or perhaps just one, littering the grass. Back then, would one empty bottle make him think the park dirty? Would he have been bothered by an empty bottle, or a plastic bag, while he was with her?

There was the cheap but spacious hotel room where she had given him a present. She had said, 'It's not much,' and to him her present had been the definition of 'not much'. He unwrapped the small object and exclaimed, 'This is perfect! This is the perfect present!' It was the white egg cup that now sits on the desk in his study, where he keeps pins and paper clips.

He cannot recall why Jean-Louis Guitard was in Carcassonne. Guitard was from Antibes-les-Bains – that he remembers precisely – and lived in a suburb of Paris. His work was shown in a gallery on Rue Mouffetard. Was Guitard still working on his next exhibition in Carcassonne? Had he been invited, given a residency? In those days, he would not have asked an artist questions about practical matters, such as residential arrangements an artist might benefit from (he didn't yet know what an artist-in-residence was). Now, having known many painters, and in his fifties, he knows that Guitard would have most likely been proud of being an invited artist, and would have most likely appreciated being asked and talking about it. But as a young man, wanting to understand how one becomes an artist, why one is an artist, his questions always kept the artist's practical considerations at bay; they were of a more philosophical nature. He wanted to reach the essence of the artist's life, not its practicalities. Now he understands that, of course, practical considerations are as important in an artist's life as the artist's inner necessities.

In the spacious, cheap hotel room, he had opened the wardrobes and the bathroom door. The bathroom was old, probably from the 1920s, and had a long bathtub…

He placed the egg cup on the bedside table on the right-hand side of the bed, closer to the bathroom.

'Will you be sleeping on that side of the bed?' she asked, smiling.

He smiled back.

'I suspect,' she continued, 'that we will change sides during the night and that you might wake on a different side.'

He smiled again.

'That is, if you sleep at all,' she added. And this was when he went around the room, opened the wardrobe doors, and looked into the bathroom.

The room had a faint smell of mould. He had opened the tall windows, which looked out over the river and, beyond it, the small park.

She was dressed in black jeans and a tight black sweater. It was late afternoon. She stripped down to her white lace bra and underpants. Undressing to his underwear was not something he could do in her presence.

'I'm going to take a bath,' she said, crossing the room to the bathroom and closing the door behind her. He heard the water running into the bathtub.

He lay on the bed, looking at the ceiling, at the mould stains on the plaster. In his mind he saw her again in her underwear and was trying to figure out whether she was beautiful or not. When he met her at the train station in the morning, he had found her beautiful enough. Now in her underwear, was she his idea of a beautiful girl? Her shoulders were a little narrow and round, and the lower part of her hips a little broad. Her breasts were round and high, but small. She had crossed the room in her underwear, looking at him, and he had avoided looking at her.

Still, as he thought of her while staring at the high ceiling, he became aroused. Instead of finding answers in his arousal, he became annoyed by his inability to control his urges and analyse his feelings in peace.

Then she called out: 'Why don't you come and rub my back?'

Now what was he going to do with his obvious erection? He decided to wait until it passed, but it was not passing. She called out again and he answered that, yes, he was coming, soon. The longer he lay there on the bed, waiting, the harder his penis got inside his trousers. So he got up and stood at the window for a moment, watching the ducks on the river and a middle-aged couple strolling through the park, before he went to open the bathroom door.

She was naked, of course, but thick foam almost hid her body, except for parts of her breasts. She was sitting in the tub rather than lying deep in it, as he had expected. Her nudity, though partly hidden, overwhelmed him. How was he, standing there before her, to control the response of his young man's body to her nudity? His erection, which had softened a little at the window, hardened again instantly.

'How can this happen when I don't even desire her clearly?' he thought, seeing his penis protruding obscenely in his trousers.

He sat on the side of the bath, slightly behind her, and with a bath glove began gently rubbing her shoulders.

He remembers that they talked. He cannot remember what they talked about, but he remembers relaxing as they talked, becoming less conscious of his sexual conundrum and of the erection he was so eager to conceal. He had not wanted to pass for a sexual being to her, he recalls his young self's thinking with a smile; to her, he wanted to be an intellectual being she would admire.

That night in bed, they kissed. They kissed all night and hardly slept. Several times he came in his underwear. Now, past fifty, he sees that even as he had come, his desire never waned; he kept kissing her and fondling her breasts, bottom, and hips. He could have made love to her all night. There were moments when they lay on their sides, facing each other and touching each other's skin, softly.

They didn't make love. She never touched his penis, and he can't remember placing his hand on her pubis, though he probably did, and most likely she removed it. He remembers pressing his penis, through his boxer shorts, between her legs, against her wet pubis in her white lace underpants. He remembers the bitter smell of their sweat and of her wetness. He remembers her rubbing her pubis against his penis. This was how he came many times. On top of her or her on top of him. He remembers her on top of him, having rolled him onto his back. They had closed the shutters, but light from the street came into their room through the slits, and in the dimness her white underwear seemed to glow.

He dozed off at dawn, not long before her watch beeped a few times. When he opened his eyes, he saw her in her underwear at the window, looking down at the small park and the river below.

§

Guitard was bald and wore glasses with large black frames, which were not in fashion at the time.

He wore a loose black silk shirt with the sleeves rolled up, and white trousers. At first, he thought that Guitard wore the colours he used in his ink drawings. He felt compelled to ask at once whether the artist ever expressed himself in colours other than black, white, and the spectrum of grey between, but he didn't.

He met Guitard at an address not far from the hotel where he and his friend were staying. It had not taken long to walk to Guitard's place. The hotel owner had explained how to get to the main crossroads; then he had got lost in the small streets before miraculously stumbling upon the workshop.

The place looked like a metalworker's workshop, with scraps of metal in the enclosed yard and thick, metal-framed windows on each side. Guitard used the workshop on one side of the yard. The workshop, he explained, had been built in the 1880s and used by a poster and card-printing company until the 1950s. They were now used by artists; another artist, a metal sculptor, worked in the other workshop on the far side of the yard. 'He makes tables hanging from ceilings and chairs cleverly balanced,' said Guitard. 'He used to sculpt wood, but he seems to be going through a metal phase, making useful objects.'

He didn't hide his curiosity, and when he walked into Guitard's workshop he looked about him, eyes wide, and went around the long room to, one would have thought, inspect the framed drawings hanging on the walls. He spent only a few seconds, however, looking at the two or three drawings in progress on a large inclined table. He felt it was indiscreet to look at unfinished work. The opaque windows of the workshop, gridded like the pages of pupils' notebooks with thin lead lines, filtered the sunny day's light into a greyish haze, and as a result it seemed that inside the workshop it was winter.

Guitard offered him tea, which he accepted. They sat down at a small table in a corner of the room where there were no drawings, and with their tea and a few *sablés* in a saucer before them, they began to talk.

No one was in the hotel room when he came back from his meeting with Guitard. He lay down on the bed and opened the book she had left on the bedside table near the window. She had mentioned Marguerite Duras in her last letter. He started to read the first page, then the next, turned one or two more – they were short pages. He stopped soon after he had started. He stopped and fell asleep.

When he woke, it was dark, save for the light from the street that had invited itself into the far corner of the room, near the door. He went to the bathroom, then lay down again and quickly fell asleep.

Her coming back to the room had not woken him. He thinks he remembers her softly stroking his hair while he slept, and his wanting to wake, almost waking, but in the end remaining asleep as she stroked his hair. When he eventually woke, the room was as it had been when he'd first woken. Near the door he saw now a shadow projected by the street light. He recognised the shape of her body, elongated by the angle of the light, and the outline of her wavy hair down to her shoulders. She was standing at the window, dressed in her black top and trousers.

Late in the evening, he took a bath and washed his hair with bath soap. Neither of them had brought shampoo. His hair dried quickly after the bath and was soft and spiky. She kept tousling his hair, amused by how it felt to touch and at how it stood upright on his head, as if charged with electricity.

As he and Guitard sat down, he began by saying he wanted them to talk about the transfiguration of light and shadow in his work, the common thread, it seemed, in all of Guitard's art. He also wanted Guitard to tell him what an artist was, and how one became one.

He always felt awkward during these introductions, and about asking questions. He preferred simply to sit with an artist and say nothing. But today, he asked a question, one of the few he had prepared.

Guitard pondered what he had just said. His seventeen-year-old self rephrased and even expanded the question, interrupting Guitard's train of thought. It was his question about light and shadow.

'You shouldn't take what I say too literally, or some of my words might sound silly or pretentious,' warned Guitard. Then, instead of talking about light and shadow, as if he had only heard the young man's preamble, Guitard said: 'There are people who become artists, and others who are born artists. That is what happened to me, I was born an artist. I didn't know it for a number of years, but somehow I was born with a pencil in one hand and a sheet of paper in the other. When I was a child in Antibes, I'd go for walks and spend long moments before the sea, before the cape and its trees.

'My parents were separated. I was a mediocre pupil. A real dunce. But in those days there were fifty spots for forty pupils, so unless you were the most obnoxious of children, you'd move up each year. What fascinated me most, though, was the cape of Antibes and the pine trees and the sea. I had no interest in what we were told at school.

'There were no artists in the family. You know, you have to be reckless to be an artist. My family was a rather *bourgeois* family. Doctors, lawyers, business people... My grandfather had been some sort of music conductor in his spare time, but a banker by day. I tell you, my parents were very sorry when I announced I was going to be an artist!'

He slapped the table with both palms, and the teacups, saucers, and spoons in the saucers trembled. 'Very sorry!' he said again, with a burst of laughter.

'When I was a kid, I found the shadow of someone walking in the street beautiful. It ravished me. I was… aaaah.' He lofted his eyes as if thanking the heavens, a broad grin across his round face. He looked at the young man, the grin still wide.

'On my way somewhere,' continued Guitard, 'I would stop to look at what I found beautiful. And I found almost everything beautiful.

'There have been a number of epiphanies, or what I'd rather call "shocks". Regular shocks, if you like. To me, an epiphany is a realisation. These moments were more like unexpected problems that stopped me from getting on with my life.

'There were no art books at home, but the family read the papers. *Nice-Matin* and *L'Espoir*. One of the papers printed *The Adventures of Professor Nimbus*. Professor Nimbus was a little man, a scientist of sorts, who wore a tailcoat and was bald. I'm bald, but I have hair around my temples. Nimbus was completely bald – except for one hair on the top of his head in the shape of a question mark. One day, reading a Professor Nimbus story, I said to myself, What is going on? I was six or seven. It's funny what can go on in the head of a six- or seven-year-old. I suddenly realised that Nimbus was drawn with a line. I thought that fact strange. People didn't have a line around them, around their faces. My mother, my sisters, no one I knew had such a line. Nimbus did. I asked my grandmother, "Why does Nimbus have a line around him and not you?" And my grandmother gave a rather definite answer, she said, "Because."

‘I couldn’t shake the question off; as I drew, it was always at the back of my mind. I was constantly drawing. I went from sketching cowboys to sketching my friends and what I saw on my walks around Antibes. Subconsciously, I was bothered by the lines I traced around people and things, when no such line actually existed. I must draw without drawing a line around things, I kept saying to myself… This question of the line was a problem when drawing, but not when painting…’

He interrupted Guitard to ask whether, when he painted, he first drew the subject or scene. Guitard said, not answering the question, ‘I place drawing on the same level as painting: a complete, fulfilling form of art, not a preparatory one. It’s a form of art in its own right, and as a child I was convinced of this, even though I never consciously formulated that idea.

‘It took me years to eliminate the line I drew around things. The line of contour. It was a slow process, a problem for years…'

He asked again about light and shadow, slightly rephrasing the question. He knew that therein lay the answer to the contour-line problem Guitard had been describing. He wanted Guitard to know he knew.

'You know, I'm not an intellectual being; I'm more of a sensory being. What I appreciate is being with a woman I like, eating what I like, being with people whose company makes me feel good, doing what I like doing. I'm not a guy who spends his time…' He grabbed his head with both hands and leaned sideways in his chair. The chair creaked as he moved. He thought the word Guitard might have used, rather than grabbing his head, was 'intellectualising'.

'You wish for me to tell you what an artist is…' Guitard then lowered his voice and spoke more slowly: 'An artist is someone who experiences sensations and feelings about everyday life, or its smallest elements, more strongly than others.

Sometimes the smallest elements of everyday life shock the artist, whether it's a crumb of bread on the tablecloth or the explosion of an atomic bomb. Such a person is inhabited by the need to recreate or transcribe these emotions and feelings through an art form…'

He thought he should debate Guitard a little on his definition of the artist. He felt they needed to go deeper into the being of an artist. He said, 'This definition doesn't take into account the narcissistic need of those who claim to be artists…'

'Who said the artist was a narcissistic being?' asked Guitard.

He thought about it and could not find a name until he remembered Bruno Bettelheim, about whom he had just read in a magazine. He could not remember what the article had said, but he threw the name in the discussion.

'Bettelheim, for one.'

Guitard looked at him, and he didn't know whether the artist was going to laugh or shout. Guitard finally said, with jovial vehemence, 'If you keep company with these people, my friend, you're doomed. The job of psychoanalysts is to talk, to digress. Do you realise that when you speak for an hour, you'll likely utter about fifty stupidities? Imagine if your profession were to talk all of your life… Why look into everything's whys and wherefores…'

Guitard paused.

'Of course, there are narcissistic artists,' he continued in a reflective tone, gazing above the young man's head. 'We'll come back to that,' he said, now looking into the young man's eyes. 'Remind me later to come back to that.'

'An artist needs three things,' Guitard went on. 'First, the need to recreate emotions; second, to make a choice – writing poems, novels, singing songs, playing the piano, designing buildings, painting pictures, and so on – you see where I'm going; third, to develop technique. The second point, this choice I'm talking about is, of course, a subconscious one. One is a comedian because one has always been a comedian. They haven't changed, only revealed themselves. Like the man who wins the lottery and leaves his wife and children, buys a castle, and takes fifteen mistresses. People say money changed him. No, money revealed what was already inside him, for which he'd never had the means to act. In his head, he already had his fifteen mistresses. That choice leads to the form through which the artist expresses themselves.

'You express yourself through the elements that marked your environment. Your friend Bettelheim would tell you we all carry what affected us in childhood. My childhood environment was Antibes, and its light profoundly affected me.

'There were three or four years, between the age of thirteen and seventeen, during which things were decided for me. When – subconsciously – I made my choice. Without knowing it, during those years I leaned firmly towards being an artist and towards drawing. Towards the need to use light. Towards the desire to create, with light and shadow, things I saw as profound and true – things that spoke to me of the simple beauty of existence, of daily existence…'

The second night they spent together was very much like the first. That is how he remembers it. They fell asleep just before dawn, and just before noon the telephone woke them. They had to check out, the receptionist told them. When, he asked, half-asleep. Well, now, the receptionist said.

In the afternoon, wearing their sunglasses, they walked through the old city. He doesn't remember what the city looked like. They probably walked along the fortified walls; however, he cannot recall what the city looked like from the old walls. They shared a sandwich from a bakery near the hotel, sitting on a bench in the small park after checking out and before walking around the old town. It was a hot day, and he wore a T-shirt. She probably wore something different that day, but he remembers her in her black trousers and tight long-sleeved black top.

In the old town stood a small Roman church, and when they approached it, she said she wanted to go inside. Inside, it was cool and deserted. He sat on a bench in the middle of the nave. He looked around. It was an old church, like any other. Then he closed his eyes.

When he opened his eyes, he didn't think he had dozed off. His friend was sitting two or three rows in front of him. He waited a long time for her to turn and look for him. She didn't. They sat there, motionless. He closed his eyes again and fell asleep.

When they walked out of the church, the sun

was hidden behind some of the taller surrounding buildings. He asked her if she had fallen asleep while they were sitting inside. She said no.

'…all that I see, all that I sense, all that I find beautiful – and I find almost everything beautiful – is amplified within me because I know, because I feel in my gut, that I'm going to die.' Guitard paused. He could no longer detect the tremors of humour in Guitard's voice.

Guitard waved his right arm in a semicircle, glancing vaguely around the workshop. 'All this will only last a very short while.'

Guitard was now waving at what was outside, at everything. Inexplicably, his seventeen-year-old self felt uneasy.

'Things pass at terrifying speed.' Guitard looked at him with a new intensity. He saw in the artist's eyes a kind of despair, but he also saw the cape of

Antibes and its pine trees. The sea. He saw himself in the sea, lost in infinite space.

'You are twenty, maybe. I don't know – twenty-two, twenty-five. Do you realise you've passed that time? It won't come back. It's gone. Did you see it pass?'

He had never contemplated time in that way, never *felt* mortality through time, though he had read philosophers who wrote about it. He thought of Charles Aznavour's song about youth, *Sa Jeunesse*, his only visceral experience of the passing of time. His jaw clenched. He could not talk.

Guitard whistled. 'You'll get to seventy,' he said smiling broadly. 'You'll laugh and think: everything's passed, it's all gone!

'Everyone knows this, yet no one *feels* it,' said Guitard, his voice suddenly loud. 'I first felt it in the deepest corner of my gut when I was fourteen. On the beach between Le Ponteil and La Salis. It was then a beach of rocks and wrack, not the neat, tourist beach it is today. I was on that beach, sitting on the rocks, contemplating the cape, the parasol pines, the villas… One day, I'll stop seeing this, I said to myself. The chapel of La Garoupe, the villas, the sea splashing against the rocks. All of this will continue to exist, but one day I'll no longer be here to see it. A new fear took hold of me. There.' He poked his stomach several times with his right index finger.

'I was terrified. From the height of my fourteen years, I felt my body empty itself. I was in my swimmers on those rocks – it was summer – and I broke out in a cold sweat.

'That fear has never left me. Every day, I feel the same sensation I felt on those rocks in Antibes at fourteen. I've rarely talked about it. You don't talk about these things when you're trying to be a man, you know what I mean? The day you stop caring about being a bloke, there's no longer any shame in talking about such fears. Every day this fear visits me, accompanied by vertigo. Often in the evening. The fear of nothingness, my drawings, that's what they are. This fear multiplies the beauty of things. I draw. Rather than put a gun to my head, I draw. In the street, there are such beautiful things: three cobblestones, a small leaf of grass between them, grey cobblestones, green leaf of grass, the sun is out and I stare at the stones and the grass for over a quarter of an hour.'

What he felt that day in front of Guitard, what started in his stomach and spread through his body, was akin to what Guitard had felt on the rocks of the Antibes beach. And like Guitard's fear, his own has never left him; to this day it still visits him. Although it lives within him, the fear has the presence of a visitor. It has mostly visited him in the night, in his dreams or in his insomnia.

§

Back home, he didn't know what to do. His desk, with its small, low-density lamp and photos of Guitard's drawings, was not inviting. The owner of the Rue Mouffetard gallery had left several messages on his answering machine, asking when she could expect to read the piece on Guitard. The deadline was the end of the month; she needed the catalogues printed the following month.

From his bed, which, in his studio apartment, stood against the right side of the desk, he worked on the Guitard piece. He had moved the desk lamp so it lit his bed, as he often did when reading at night.

It was laborious. At first, he didn't know where to start. Then he thought that somehow he had to start – he had no choice – and so he did, but later wondered whether he should have started somewhere else. He started over, decided not to begin a third time, and resolved to continue no matter what. He continued, but it was hard; his mind could not focus on themes or ideas. He went back to his notes, but they were only notes, not developed ideas, analysis, or even basic descriptions of Guitard's work. His notes were in a red notebook, where he had also written about his friend after she had taken the train back to Montpellier from Carcassonne station. He had gone back to the bench in the park by the river and written down things he thought might matter later. Now, lying in bed, they still didn't seem to matter. Not yet. Perhaps because he had written them not long before, they didn't seem to offer anything revealing or true. Later, in several years perhaps, they might.

He continued working on the Guitard piece, slowly, over the next two weeks, and sent a typewritten draft by post to the gallery owner. He received a call from her several days later, which he didn't answer. She said on the answering machine that the piece was very good, that she had made minor edits and sent him a cheque. She hoped he would attend the *vernissage* the following month. Guitard would be pleased to see him again, she added.

While slowly working on the Guitard piece in bed, he had started several letters to his friend, trying to talk about Carcassonne and what he had felt after his nap in the church. He found the first draft too sentimental and burnt it with the flame of the candle he kept on his desk. For the second, he turned to Nietzsche and Bachelard, paraphrasing some of their texts on passion and dreams. He burnt that draft too because he didn't want to paraphrase anyone in his letters to her, and she might have realised he had paraphrased Nietzsche, since she had introduced him to him. It was a shame, the Nietzsche- and Bachelard-inspired letter had been very good. It said what he had wanted to say. He wrote several other drafts, all of which left him unhappy. In the end, after a month back in his apartment, he sent a routine letter about what he had read or seen that month. He thought of sending her the piece on Guitard, but decided that would be presumptuous and that she might not find it good

She wrote back with a routine letter too. A beautiful one.

It strikes him, as he rereads that letter, that he and she saw beauty in small things rather than big ones, as, in fact, Guitard had. They were unable to talk about big things, only the small ones. To him, Carcassonne had been a big thing, and he could not then say anything meaningful or essential about it. She seemed to suffer from the same affliction, though he's unsure whether Carcassonne had been a big thing for her. He tends to believe it had.

§

Two or three months later, the gallery owner left a message asking him to meet a realist Hungarian painter living in Paris, named Sandorfi. She added that it was a shame he had not made it to Guitard's opening. Guitard had asked about him, said he had liked the piece in the catalogue, and had been surprised to learn he was only seventeen (he was now eighteen).

He called back, thanked her, and wrote down Sandorfi's address. He was to meet him the following Tuesday, at seven in the evening.

By then, his hair was longer, and he had a patchy black beard.

That day, he rearranged his desk, pushing his university papers into a pile on one side, and the draft letters to his friend, with the books he had been using or mentioning in those letters, to the other. The leather folding desk mat his aunt had given him was now cleared so he could place photographs of Sandorfi's paintings on it.

The following Tuesday evening, he took the suburban train to Paris, then the métro to Vaugirard. Sandorfi lived on the sixth floor of a *Haussmanien* building in the fifteenth arrondissement.

A striking young *métisse* woman, wearing a short black silk dressing gown, opened the door when he rang. She led him to the kitchen, where Sandorfi was eating a croissant and drinking black coffee. She left them together.

'Would you like a croissant?' offered Sandorfi, in a soft, almost inaudible voice.

'No, thank you.' His own voice sounded ten times louder than Sandorfi's. More softly, he asked, 'Would you prefer I come back another time?'

Sandorfi looked at him, perplexed. 'Didn't we say seven?'

'We did.'

Sandorfi kept looking at him. Then said, 'It is past seven, no? So it's fine.'

The painter, reluctantly, it seemed to the young man, explained that he went out to nightclubs most nights for a few hours, came home at daybreak, slept, got up when it was dark, and painted until about three in the morning before starting again.

Sandorfi stood. He wore a long grey silk dressing gown. 'Let's get to work,' he said, in a whisper.

They went into a large, unfurnished room. The apartment, from what he had seen, seemed sparsely furnished. From the front door to the kitchen, then to the painter's workspace, he had walked down a dark corridor, where he had glimpsed a navy-blue couch in one room and an unmade futon with a single sheet in another. In the room where Sandorfi worked, the young métisse woman sat naked on an old wooden chair.

Sandorfi fetched a wooden chair from another room and placed it beside his easel. He gestured for the young man to sit. Sandorfi began working on the canvas, standing.

His younger self shifted the chair so he faced Sandorfi and the easel, not the naked woman.

He cannot remember his discussion with Sandorfi. The painter's whispers and gentle accent have almost vanished; only his movements remain precisely in memory.

The painter was impassive, his movements slow. He can almost hear the whisper of the silk gown's loose sleeves, like a faint breath that sometimes brushed the canvas.

He remembers the apartment to be of the same colours and tones as the paintings. There was an obscurity trapped in it – the woman, the sheet she was to wrap herself in, the walls, the roughly polished wooden floor, which had no patina, all appeared darker because of it. Paradoxically, the act of painting the woman and the objects had illuminated that obscurity. Sandorfi painted with little light, at night, yet his paintings, like the silk paintings he saw in Japan years later, were somehow brilliant. Sandorfi himself was the source of light on the obscure scene he was painting.

He doesn't own any works by Guitard or Sandorfi. He wishes he did. He still has a copy of Guitard's catalogue and drafts of the essay he wrote about Sandorfi's work, which the gallery owner rejected (though she paid him for it). She had told him she felt the Nietzsche references were inappropriate, and that his essay had been vague, she had not been sure what he had meant, and had not found it related clearly to Sandorfi or his work, despite the mentions of the painter and his precise descriptions.

He had known she was right. He thought a lot about the essay back then. He could not figure out why he had failed. He knew why it had been rejected – the reasons were those the gallery owner had given

– but he did not know what had led him to write such an essay.

For months, he barely wrote. A few short letters to his friend. The gallery owner didn't call again, but that didn't bother him. He studied a little, but his desk didn't feel right for studying. The two candles stayed there, unlit. He lay on his bed and watched television. He read a little. He opened Nietzsche at random on two or three occasions but felt betrayed by the philosopher after reading a few paragraphs. Each paragraph felt familiar, and therefore disappointing. He decided not to open Nietzsche again for a while.

He opened Schopenhauer, Heidegger, Husserl and Merleau-Ponty. Then Spinoza, Montaigne, Alain, and Bachelard. They were his old friends. But he closed them soon after opening them. He could no longer read Althusser or Ricœur, his favourite contemporary philosophers, nor could he read

Levinas. He could read Kierkegaard and still manage some Serres. But he grew bored with them, and one day, in early spring, he felt depressed at the prospect of not being able to read. Then, at some point early in the university break, he stopped reading altogether, and wrote nothing.

He spent the holidays in his studio apartment, trying to figure things out.

One day, on the suburban train, he saw a young woman reading a book titled *The Joke*. Another day, he saw a young man reading a book called *A Man Asleep*. He knew these books were novels. He remembered then his friend had read all of Duras's books. Duras wrote novels. So, one day, he looked for novels on the bookshelves in his studio and at his parents' house. But there were none.

He went to the municipal library and looked for *The Joke*. *The Joke*, even if a novel, would certainly develop philosophical themes, with such a title, he expected. Once, he had written an essay for the university philosophy journal on laughter. Perhaps then he should have read *The Joke* as research.

He found the book. On the cover, as on the book he had seen the young woman reading on the train, only the author's surname was printed. It looked promising, he thought, and he took the book home.

At the library, he had not opened the book to see what was inside. He opened it a few days later, at home. He was still hesitant about reading a novel. How much truth about anything can one really find in a novel?

Reading *The Joke* made him happy. He went back to the library and borrowed *A Man Asleep*. It was a short book, and he read it in an afternoon. He kept the curtains closed and read it in bed. The 'man asleep' was him. He might as well have written the book himself, since it told his story.

He went back to the library. On that occasion, he

spent a long time there, the whole morning, looking at what some of the other novels were about. He thought of reading other books by the authors of *The Joke* and *A Man Asleep*, but decided to keep them for later. They were good to read.

He saw a thick book. A thick book ought to be a serious one, he thought, and he borrowed it.

The thick book had two effects on him: first, it made him want to write to his aunt to tell her about the books, the novels, he had read, and to ask if he might visit and borrow more from her (he didn't write to her); second, it made him copy paragraphs from it into his next letter to his friend.

In the thick book, the author described a dog walking down a street. It was revealing. He saw the scene in black and white, visualising it as a drawing by Guitard.

That scene, of the dog walking, was a 'shock', he now knows.

He copied it into a letter to his friend. He didn't tell her it wasn't his; he passed it off as his own description of a dog walking down the street. His next letters were full of paragraphs, sometimes even chapters, from novels he had borrowed from the library. The novels made him happy to be reading again. Not all pleased him, but even those he found mediocre somehow assured him of something, of what, he wasn't sure.

Could he write a novel? he wondered one day. Yes, he could, he thought. In fact, the novel was already laid out before him. He could describe the moments he had spent with his friend in Carcassonne, his meeting with Guitard, and so on. It was all there. The only rule was that, tempting as it might be, he could not, should not, copy others.

One evening, he sat at his desk and began to write the novel. He tentatively titled it *Voyage à Carcassonne*. It was good to have a title, it made beginning the novel easier. He started well, he wrote a few hundred words in an hour or so. It was easy, much easier than writing essays. And it was fast. He filled a few pages of a large notebook. The scenes about Guitard came out as if he were reliving them in the present moment. And he smiled as he wrote, and he laughed when Guitard laughed. And he forgot the music playing softly in the background of his apartment. Rather, the music encouraged him in a subtle way, he felt it flowed with his writing. And he heard the music again, somehow, as he wrote about the 'shocks', and wondered whether he was experiencing one.

Later that evening, he let out a cry. A cry of success, of excitement, who knows. He was with his friend again, in the hotel room in Carcassonne, and it was good. As good as when they had been there.

He wrote about the park and the bench where they had sat. His mind was spinning. Writing was intoxicating, he remembers.

He wrote about the church, the old town, then taking his friend to the station, and being alone. His eyes grew tired. It was the middle of the night, he guessed. He thought now that he should write about what had happened after Carcassonne. The letters he could not write, the depression that had followed, the struggle to read. Not reading. Not writing. But he thought he should get to that later, tomorrow. He was two-thirds through his novel, he estimated, and went to bed.

He woke at midday the following day and went straight to his novel on the desk. It was five or six pages long. It wasn't a novel, but that didn't bother him; as he reread it, he found it very good. Even rested and lucid, without music, as he reread it, he was transported back to Carcassonne, to the hotel room, and to Guitard's workshop. He continued, and by evening it was close to ten pages long. It was a short story.

Without waiting to decide whether it was wise, he typed it up and sent it to his friend. Typed, it came to six pages.

§

His friend's response didn't arrive straight away. Either the six-page manuscript had taken longer than a normal letter to reach her, or she was taking her time to respond.

His friend had been reading novels and stories for much longer than he had. While waiting for her response to his short story, he worried that she had found his writing uninteresting, or even bad. He reread the story several times but could not convince himself it was bad. His friend probably didn't know what to say about it and was taking her time to work something out. That is what he figured. He had come to be certain that a six-page text and cover letter wouldn't take longer than a normal letter to reach the south of the country. That much was clear to him.

Then a response came. By the time it arrived, he had come to expect a long critique of his story, not necessarily negative, but detailed. His friend read a lot and liked to talk about what she read. She could write several pages about a book. He expected a review of his story similar to the reviews she wrote of the books she read.

The letter was, for the most part, a beautiful routine one; then, at the end, before signing with her usual 'A.', she wrote: 'The writing in your story reminds me of Marguerite Duras's.' That was all. Was it good? Was it bad? She had said practically nothing about his story.

He felt the comparison with Duras had more to do with her reading than with his writing. She had found nothing to say about the story and had expressed her love for Duras rather than her thoughts on his story. Duras, he knew, was the centre of his friend's literary universe – she was dazzled by the older woman's writing.

He was disappointed. The thought of going to the library to borrow Duras's books passed, and instead he reread *Voyage à Carcassonne*.

Much later, when he and his friend were no longer friends, he read all of Duras's books and while reading Duras, he thought of his friend. Then he read about Duras and thought of his friend even more. Her life and Duras's had uncanny similarities. Perhaps that was why Duras had been so important to her.

He couldn't remember where his friend had been born, but she had spent her childhood on the French Caribbean island of Martinique, without a father, with her younger brother, both brought up by their mother, a schoolteacher.

Marguerite Duras was born and spent her childhood in the French colony of Cochinchina, without a father, with her two brothers, Pierre and Paulo, the three brought up by their mother, a schoolteacher.

Duras adored her younger brother and loathed her elder one; his friend loved her brother one day and hated him the next.

From the age of fifteen, Duras had lovers, starting with the 'North China lover'. From the age of fifteen, his friend had lovers. All different from one another. Young ones, older ones. He had known about the delivery man from the furniture shop and the philosophy professor, and the singer. Another of her lovers, he remembers, worked at the school canteen, and another lived next door with his wife and two children.

Although he has not developed the fervour for Duras that his friend and others had, he has enjoyed reading her books. Unlike Zola or, say, Solzhenitsyn, he read Duras while lying in bed, sometimes with his wife asleep at his side. During weekends away or at home. He encouraged his wife to read Duras. He even told his wife once that, should she learn French, Duras could be a good author to try reading in French.

But, of course, as he read Duras's books, his imagination always placed his friend's face in place of Duras's, or her female characters.

§

His next birthday was soon approaching. Carcassonne was now almost two years in the past. He still thought of Guitard, from time to time, and of that fear that he had described to him. He wondered whether that fear was routinely with him, as it had been with

Guitard. He thought he could feel it most days but some days he thought it was not really there.

Now he sees that his almost nineteen-year-old self was quite aware of his mortality but not as profoundly as his fifty-something-year-old self.

Mortality is like a retirement plan: many things remind you that you have to consider it seriously, but it is only as you grow older that you begin to consider it seriously. He smiles at the analogy. More often now he senses that one day, in *his* lifetime, will be the day before his retirement day.

Then, he still waited for his friend's letters, and every day he checked his letterbox. His letters to her had somehow become shorter. It seemed he had less to say to her.

The story about Carcassonne had replaced Carcassonne. When he thought of Carcassonne, he thought of her and the facts from the story rather than the real her and the real facts, which were considerably different.

He didn't remember then the impression that had inhabited him when he had awoken from the sleep in the church, but it was that impression, he was now certain, that had pushed him to write the Carcassonne story.

Now he remembered that he and his friend, in the hotel room, on the bench in the park, in the old city, had been as close as two beings could be. Yet, before he took her to the train station, he had yearned to be inside her. In the church he had dreamt that his mind had moved into her mind, and his body into her body. He had felt it had been more than a dream. But what? Wasn't it simply desire dressed up as a dream?

He had desperately wanted to know her, to feel her emotions, think her thoughts, so he could be with her, and she with him, without a single hesitation. To his young self, that was the only relationship he wished to be in. The Carcassonne story told the story of the love for his friend and the attempt of his younger self to elevate it to where it could not be elevated.

And back then Carcassonne was a story he had published in the university literary journal, and three students had written to him to say they admired it. One of the students became his girlfriend and the next summer he moved in with her. Her apartment was bigger and closer to the university than his.

He was now preparing a letter to his friend to tell her he was about to move in with a young woman, that he was soon to have a new address. He had two months to write it.

The day of his nineteenth birthday, as he expected, he received one piece of mail. From her. It was a small parcel with his address in her handwriting on the padded envelope. He opened it slowly, meticulously, to make sure that he did not rip any part of the letter or anything inside. The small parcel contained a book from the Folio collection and a letter from her. The book was by a Japanese author he had not read. This was how the book started: 'Ever since my childhood, Father had often spoken to me about the Golden Temple...'

No one called him that evening. His parents and girlfriend had called him in the morning and the few friends he counted most likely didn't know it was his birthday, so he kept reading and finished the book without interruption.

The Holiday House

His parents owned a holiday house in the resort town of Cap d'Agde until he was about twelve, when they sold it so his father could buy a new car and pay for flying lessons. Later, with money left from the house's sale, his father bought a share in a small Cessna with three friends. They sold the plane a year or two later, after almost crashing in the English Channel one stormy night. His father still tells the story of that near-fatal night. He had been one of two pilots; the other two friends sat behind him and Jean-Pierre Huré. How many times has his father said he had never sweated so much in his life, hanging on with superhuman strength to the control column to stop the plane dropping like an inert object? *Trou d'air* is an expression he can relate only to his father's story; he would never use it to describe anything other than the turbulence in that story. Whenever he heard the expression, he was brought back to the small cockpit where his father and three friends saw death in the form of a storm.

Many times he has tried to imagine what it would feel like to be in a small plane dropping out of the sky. How could one not give up, close one's eyes, and welcome death? He would have given up; he wouldn't have screamed, but he would have closed his eyes, smiled, tried not to think of smashing into the concrete-hard sea, and concentrated on, waited for, the blissful embrace, whatever awaited him once his body was dislocated, made one with the wreck of the Cessna… But his father, according to the story, never for a moment contemplated abandoning the fight with the elements.

He has seen his father sweat, when they played tennis together, for instance, and he would say to himself: This is nothing compared to the night he flew back from Guernsey with Jean-Pierre Huré and the other two friends whose names have vanished from the story. That night he sweated more than ever, and never again would he sweat so much, certainly not playing tennis with me.

He doesn't remember questioning his father about that night over the stormy English Channel. The story, as told by his father, was final; it contained all there was to know. Except how his father had felt when the plane dropped. As a child, the story fascinated him but also unnerved him. His father had described how, for what seemed an eternity, the plane fell. He and Jean-Pierre Huré managed to bring it back under control, lift its nose a little, before the storm shook the minuscule craft with the four men inside and let it drop again – again and again, it seemed. It seemed it would never end.

He doesn't think of it as a story about how he might have lost his father, but as a story of his father's heroics, his loyal friend Jean-Pierre Huré, tennis and card partner turned co-pilot, at his side. For him, the story has remained the story he received as a child. He has never attempted to make sense of it as an adult.

Two or three years after the Cessna trip to the Channel Islands, a catchy Jacques Higelin song played on the radio. 'Tombé du ciel' – 'fallen from the sky'. And He remembers his father and Jean-Pierre Huré, tipsy at dinner or during card games, randomly launching into the song – *Tombé du ciel à travers les nuages…* Why was it that, in these quiet moments, after the cards had been dealt and each player was sorting their hand, forming a game plan, his father puffing on his cigar, they would start humming 'Tombé du ciel'? Behind the silent appreciation of the cards they had been dealt, what were their thoughts? Was a buried anxiety lurking? A memory stirred? A primal fear woken by a bad hand? They would conclude their little choir after a line or two, just as the round began.

Number 21 at the *Résidence des Lauriers*. There were about forty houses at *Les Lauriers,* five of them larger and located at the top of the hill. One of the larger houses belonged to Armand and Odette, who were from the town of Nevers, in the Nièvre *département*. Armand, a retired jeweller, was short and fat and wore silver rings. Odette's hair was big and blonde.

His parents' house was in the middle of the residence: a small bathroom, a bedroom – his parents' – and a combined living, dining and kitchen area, from which a steep staircase, almost a ladder, led to the mezzanine above their room. The mezzanine was where he slept, and where, lying on his bed, he read while his parents took their nap. The living–dining area opened onto a small terrace, where his father had built a brick barbecue and coated it with the same pale pink roughcast that covered most of the houses in the residence. The terrace was tiled and bordered at the back by a line of laurel bushes that grew about fifty centimetres each year and whose flowers – white, bright pink and purple – perfumed the little house when his mother opened the shutters and French doors for the first time that year, on the first Sunday in July.

Why did they visit the holiday house only during the summer holidays? Was the drive too long for his father to consider travelling there for a long weekend or a week during the Christmas or Easter holidays? Were his parents unable to take time off from running their business outside the annual summer slowdown? They travelled to Cap d'Agde in the first week of July and drove home – a ten- to twelve-hour trip – on the 15th of August.

That last summer at the house, he read several *Langelot* spy novels. In previous summers, he had read *Pif* magazine. He was now too old for Pif the dog. That last summer, during his parents' nap, he had also flicked through an issue of *Lui* magazine. He kept the magazine under his mattress – precisely in the middle of the bed – so his mother wouldn't find it when she changed the sheets. He had bought the *Lui* at the nearby newsagent, while running an errand for his father's Wilde Havana cigars and his mother's Peter Stuyvesant Menthol cigarettes. He'd taken his backpack to smuggle the magazine home. His mother had been amused to see him leave the house with his backpack to buy the usual tobacco. She hadn't asked any questions. She must have thought he simply liked walking about with his new backpack.

At school, boys openly talked about girls and shared, sometimes exchanged, magazines. He had felt a deep discomfort listening to Charles's or Alexis's stories about masturbation. The last thing he wanted was to take one of their magazines home. In any case, he had no magazine to exchange. That summer, he'd bought his own magazine, a *Lui*. He didn't have to talk to any friends about it. He felt no desire to trade it or build a collection; he was content with his *Lui*. It was now part of his private world, and he would never talk to anyone about it, about what was in it.

Two years before that last summer in Cap d'Agde, his parents had befriended the family in house 15. They were from the Alsace region, from a small town called Sélestat, and they had an accent. They had three children: their daughter, Claudia, a year younger than him, and the small twin boys, three years younger, with the blondest hair. The Alsatian family had spent the previous summer at another resort, and when he saw Claudia and her brothers again that year, they seemed to have doubled in height. Claudia was a little taller than him. She had grown breasts, and her lips were slightly fuller. She was no longer the squinty girl he remembered from the photo of her and him on the terrace, taken by his parents two years earlier. There was a mystery about her, perhaps even something faintly menacing. When the two families reunited one evening at his house, he was sat next to her at dinner but felt no desire to speak to her. And she said nothing to him, didn't even look at him. He spoke at length with the twins. They laughed together at the tiny white maggots they had spotted in their pasta, and at the adults' puzzlement over how the maggots had survived the boiling. Had they come from the pack of pasta left in the cupboard of the shuttered house all year? Or from the cheese bought earlier that day and grated over the pasta? Claudia's face showed no amusement; she ate her pasta unperturbed.

His family and the Alsatians favoured different beaches; he doesn't remember any discussion among the adults about changing their habits to spend time together during the day. So they met for an apéritif and dinner once or twice a week. One day, after the beach and showers, his mother told him that she had arranged for him and Claudia to go roller-skating together. He knew the place – a large helicopter pad near the Tourist Information Office, where you could hire roller-skates. It was on the way to the shops, and he and his mother had sometimes stopped to watch the skaters. His mother had suggested he try, but he'd refused each time; he knew he'd fall the moment the skates were on his feet.

When he and his mother arrived, Claudia was already circling the rink; she waved to them. She rolled past with ease and speed, turned around in a flash, and stopped in front of them. His mother said hello. He looked around but couldn't see her parents;

her brothers weren't at the rink either. She was alone. She said hello and kept on skating. His mother led him by the hand to the office, where the attendant exclaimed at the size of his feet compared to his height as he tried on the skates. Like a newborn calf, he hesitantly took a few steps from the office to the rink. On the smooth tar of the rink, the skates seemed to take control of his legs; they suddenly moved, as if his brain had ordered a running motion, and he fell on his back. His mother cried out to ask if he was all right. He didn't answer. He got up and stood still, trying to control every muscle in his body so that none would flex, move, or even make its existence felt. He breathed as if breathing itself could make him fall, as if he'd forbidden himself to breathe – long, soft breaths.

Claudia was now in front of him. He could look into her eyes. With the skates, they were somehow the same height, though her slender figure and long arms gave him the impression she was still taller, that she would always be taller. But when he looked straight at her, it was her eyes his fell on. She smiled, the right corner of her mouth lifting. The wind from her skating had ruffled her hair; her fringe was less straight, now slightly parted on her forehead.

She took his left hand. His eyes widened, his muscles woke and tensed immediately, sensing that the unexpected movement of his arm was a prelude to another fall.

She pulled him gently, and he moved forward, trying to stay upright. For a few seconds he kept his balance, and for a few more. He began to breathe more fully, as his body demanded. She turned, glanced at his legs and laughed before looking ahead again, pulling him a little harder, the distance between them now the length of their outstretched arms. She pushed harder with her legs to gain a little speed. He looked at her back. Her left arm moved with extra force to propel them both forward.

Her body was long-limbed and slender. His eyes couldn't help falling to her lower back and hips. Strangely, their shape seemed to replicate Olivia's. He knew Olivia's body intimately, having studied it over the past four or five days during early-afternoon siestas, before the second trip to the beach. Olivia's arms and legs weren't as thin as Claudia's, but the shape of her hips, bottom, and even breasts looked identical.

From his *Lui*, he remembers only Olivia. She was on the cover. He doesn't remember the other girls from that issue.

Olivia had looked at him, smiled, and he'd felt like smiling back. She was in a magazine, but she wasn't famous, she hadn't been seen anywhere else. She was unlikely ever to be seen again. Other girls in *Lui* had probably looked at him too. What had made him want to smile back at Olivia and not the others? Why is it that, even today, he still remembers her so well, and that she and Claudia have become co-conspirators in that summer's heartbreak?

On the skating rink, he'd grown nervous realising that Claudia and Olivia shared physical traits, traits that, in the privacy of his mezzanine bedroom, had aroused him. Then, somehow remembering, or perhaps grasping subconsciously, one fear calling another, he realised he couldn't skate; his legs, as before, went into an uncontrollable, comic motion. His upper body thrust forward in a battle with his legs to keep his balance. Now his upper body jerked back. When he realised he no longer held Claudia's hand, he saw his legs in front of him, the old skates on his feet, their wheels spinning in the air, the blue sky above, he had fallen backwards.

He sat on the rink as teenagers moved past him. Claudia stood in her tight denim shorts and pale green T-shirt, its short sleeves rolled up so it looked like a singlet. She offered her right hand, palm open to the sky. She said something like, Come on, let's go, and he took her hand; pulling on her arm as she pulled him back, he managed to stand.

§

On his bedside table at the holiday house sat a small pile of three *Langelot* novels from the *Bibliothèque Verte* collection. They might have been *Langelot Agent Secret, Langelot et les Exterminateurs,* and *Langelot et la Danseuse.* Those are some of the titles he remembers. It could have been three others; it might have been a smaller pile with two, or a taller one with four. He had picked his first *Langelot* from the book section of the local newsagent one Wednesday afternoon, when his mother went to buy the following week's television guide. She had seen how dedicatedly he was reading – What are you doing in your bedroom all afternoon? I'm reading, leave me alone! – and she began buying other volumes from the newsagent or supermarket until, when he was about fourteen, he owned and had read all forty books in the series. Had his mother kept track of what he'd read? How had she remembered which ones she'd already bought? Where is his *Langelot* collection today? What did his mother do with it? Has she kept it in a box in the garage? Did she give them to one of his younger cousins when he left France for Australia, all those years ago? He hasn't seen them on the bookshelves in his childhood bedroom during recent visits. The hallway to his old bedroom still holds the hundreds of *S.A.S.* novels his father has collected, and nothing else. The covers of the *S.A.S.* books always featured half-naked women holding weapons. He'd once asked his father why he kept all those cheap-looking paperbacks instead of clearing the narrow hallway of them. His father had said that, since he owned every volume in the series, the collection was worth a lot of money. Are you planning to sell them? he'd asked. No, his father had replied. So it doesn't matter if it's worth money, he'd said. I don't understand your logic. What logic? his father had said. Why do I need logic to keep books I like, in my own house? He had replied, Aren't you the least bit embarrassed to display these badly written books, which, from the covers and the few lines I've read, seem rather sexist? Isn't there a character called Mandy la Salope? He may have been in his early thirties – perhaps late twenties – it had been during one of his early trips back to France. His father had shaken his head, smiling, and walked away.

That last summer at the Cap d'Agde holiday house, he had just started reading *Langelot*. After lunch, while his parents napped, he lay on his bed and read about the adventures of the young blond spy. He remembers Langelot being described as looking so young that his enemies often took him for a harmless adolescent before realising they faced a resourceful agent with a clear moral compass. He imagined himself taller than Langelot, even though he was only twelve or thirteen and Langelot was in his twenties; his hair wasn't blond like the spy's, it was dark brown, and he was certain his feet were longer. He resembled more closely Larry J. Bash, the hero of another series by *Langelot*'s creator, Lieutenant X. Larry J. Bash was a student at an American Ivy League university and, in his spare time, a private investigator. But it was Langelot's traits he fantasised displaying. Later – was he fourteen? – he eagerly read the adventures of Bob Morane, but Bob Morane was a man, like his father, who smelled of aftershave, whose face was square, with a squinting look and crow's-feet, and he barely saw himself in him, despite sharing his hair colour.

During his parents' nap, he read *Langelot.* But how could he immerse himself in the spy's adventures when Olivia in his *Lui* was under the mattress? When Claudia was a few doors away, or would be, upon her family's return from the beach? When would he see her again? When was the next dinner with her family planned for? Had his mother mentioned tomorrow? Later in the week? Were they not dining at Armand and Odette's tomorrow? What was it that perturbed him with Claudia? It was the first time that question, though only now does he formulate it as such, bothered him: Why am I thinking of her so much, and why am I uneasy in her company and at the same time desire it? When he was six or seven and until she changed school, he had liked Élise Gomez. He had liked Sophie Rédolfi; last year he had liked Virginie Thureau; but they had never monopolised his thoughts the way Claudia did now. He had talked to them, they had been friends, he had played with them at recess. There had been Bérangère Pagano, next to whom he had sat two years ago, and he and

Bérangère had been friends, had liked each other, and had got into trouble a few times for talking and giggling during class. Madame Constantini had raised her high-pitched voice at them so loudly that the windows had shaken.

At home, he rarely thought of Élise, Sophie or Virginie; on weekends he played tennis with Thierry Picard, invited Hervé Houdebine and other boys for play dates. Hadn't Élise Gomez been part of his group of friends who played tennis all Saturday afternoon? Why was Claudia the only thing he could think of now? Why, when he read the gripping *Langelot* stories or imagined his own adventures, when he tried to think of the beach, of the boat his father had just rented, did his mind always return to Claudia? Claudia had even pushed Olivia out of his romantic fantasies. She had conquered all of his existence.

Did he actually desire her company, or was he just curious about her? Did he feel he needed to be close enough to see the fine hair on her arms? Did he want to hold her hand, as they had at the skating rink, did he want to talk with her? Talk about what? Would he be content just to look at her from across the table, to watch her from a distance? Would he be happy to think of her at length and not know her more than he already did, to just imagine her? Did he need to share anything with her? Could she just be like Olivia in the magazine, someone he looked at, contemplated in his thoughts, who gave the appearance of looking back at him? Would he be happy to possess her as an object in his mind?

He knows he may be attributing to his twelve-year-old self questions he would only ask himself now, as a fifty-something-year-old. He has always preferred to observe people from across the table and not know them beyond those observations. Every time he has sat next to someone, got to know someone, got to desire someone, it ended…

He got to know his wife. When they met, he felt they were good for each other. The first three or four years were tumultuous. They separated seven times. She would move out – he remembers looking at her from the small window of their old bedroom as she put her bags in the boot of her brother's car, in tears. He left too, sleeping a night or two at a hotel before returning home. Once he had spent that short time separated from his wife with Hanna. The separation had just been the pretext for sleeping out, for freeing himself for a couple of nights. He always wanted to come home.

He and his wife got to know each other very well very quickly, without speaking much. He has always felt his wife could see through him. Despite the mystery of his silences, his lies, she knew what he thought. He felt that she had always known what he was doing, whom he desired, as if she had read his whole life story and psychological profile, as if she had lived with him all of her life and then come back into the past to be with him again, equipped with the knowledge of who he was, what he had done.

He and his wife got to know each other very well very quickly. Then, as if they had got too close to a burning knowledge of the other, as if the composite of what they knew intimately about each other had become unstable, they moved away from each other. They installed a distance between them. With time, that distance translated into silences, into sitting next to each other on the couch to watch the evening news and British crime dramas on television, a book moving from his bedside table to hers, a magazine switching from her hands one week to his the next, her booking a table at a restaurant and his smiling at her choice, the exchange of what anyone would judge excruciatingly common words about their respective jobs during dinners out, grew, then shrank, then grew again, naturally, until it became a kind of safety zone, from the side of which he could look at his wife, and she at him.

One evening, it was her birthday, they went out to a bar for drinks. She had just recovered from the flu and her voice was still coarse; she spoke in a deep whisper, and he looked at her and found her funny and beautiful. They followed the drinks with dinner at a French restaurant she had chosen. They were the sole diners, served by a sixty-something Australian woman whose husband was in the kitchen. Soon the husband came out with their dishes and started making conversation. Usually, he would have been very annoyed, but he saw on his wife's face that she was finding the episode amusing, so he relaxed. The chef was not French but Dutch, and drunk. The chef was very drunk that night, and he wondered how he had managed to prepare their dinner. As the chef spoke, his sentences grew nonsensical, his words so slurred they sometimes sounded like the noises of strange little animals, not quite squeaks nor quacks. He can't recall what the chef had talked about. He remembers he and his wife looking at each other, hiding their smiles, both surprisingly engaged in the strange conversation with the drunk chef whose wife was now trying to pull him back to the kitchen.

He did get to know Claudia. He knows he got to know her. Though none of it had been her doing. She had barely talked to him that last summer in Cap d'Agde, or looked at him; she had shown no curiosity in him, in what he had been up to the last two years, had shared nothing. She had laughed when he fell at the skating rink. But he had thought of her so much that summer, when they were only a few doors apart, when they saw each other as their parents dined together, and in the two or three years that followed, when he wrote to her after school and on weekends, as if what she had done to him had never happened, and she never wrote back. He still remembers Sélestat's post code.

§

He had forgotten until today about the bottle of Signoricci his mother had given him that year. The glass of the bottle was corrugated like the tin roof of his grandparents' henhouse. The bottle was shaped in an ellipse. The lid, the colour of gold, made him think of a jewel. He had got into the habit of splashing some on his neck in the morning. In Cap d'Agde, his mother had warned him not to apply any before going to the beach; exposed to the sun, the perfume, she had said, would stain his skin forever. It felt strange to go out of the house and not smell of Signoricci. He would make up for it after his shower at the end of the day. When they were out the whole day, like when his father had rented a sailboat and they had explored the coast, using mainly the boat's small engine to move, he would forget about the perfume's scent and enjoy instead the blended smells of sea and sunscreen. In the evening, his bed still rocking from the day out at sea, he would say to himself, I haven't worn any perfume today… Oh well…

One morning, Little Marc said to him, 'You smell like a girl.'

Little Marc was a year younger, short, and looking younger than he was, yet he exuded an experience of life beyond his age. He had a big laugh and he often laughed. He made jokes that amused adults; he could always capture their attention. He knew swear words he himself had never heard before, and he used them with what seemed perfect timing. With his Burgundy accent, Marc's rudeness had great comic effect. He was never rude in front of adults. In their company, he appeared the innocent child, yet still funny. His father listened and laughed at Marc's stories. He couldn't recall a time when his father had been as engaged by something *he* had said.

Little Marc was Armand and Odette's only grandson. His father had driven down to drop him off at his grandparents' for the holidays.

Now Marc sniffed the air around him noisily and asked, 'Why are you wearing perfume?'

The answer was, Because my mother bought it for me, but he thought it better to keep that to himself. He lied instead and said, 'This is my father's perfume. I borrow it from time to time.'

Marc guffawed. 'What? Your father smells like a girl too?' Then, 'Your father smells like a girl!'

He looked at Marc's face, round, with puffy cheeks, like a younger child's. His face was laughing and his eyes were closed.

His father liked Little Marc very much, and now Little Marc was making fun of his father. Marc was being unfair to him; Marc had betrayed him. What if he were to tell his father that Marc had said he smelled like a girl? Surely then Marc would lose some of the respect and affection his father had given him.

He looked at the childish face overdoing the laughter. And he wanted to punch it. Right in the puffy cheeks. On at least two occasions he had wanted to strike Thierry Picard's face, and had once done so when they were playing at Thierry's place. During a dispute over a toy they both wanted, Thierry had called him a *fils de pute.* He had looked at Thierry's face in profile for a few moments, and then punched it as hard as he could with his right hand clenched into a fist. Thierry had gone crying to his mother, who called his own mother to arrange for him to be picked up straight away. He had been horrified when Thierry had left the bedroom crying, calling, *Maman! Maman!* Horrified at the prospect of Thierry's mother scolding him in her house. In the Picard house, he was at their mercy; Madame Picard could make him feel very small. But his mother arrived quickly, before Thierry had stopped crying. She apologised, with a warm smile, and they walked home.

His mother had not asked him to apologise, she had done the apologising for him. She never revealed the incident to his father; in any case, if his father ever knew, he never mentioned it. He never got into trouble for what he'd done. Thierry avoided him at school. He remembered teasing Thierry Picard once or twice, referring to the punch and Thierry's interminable crying, and Thierry chasing him around the schoolyard but never catching him, even though, while running away, he would laugh and his laughter slowed him down. He and Thierry Picard were never friends again.

How good it would feel to punch Little Marc, as I did Thierry Picard, in the face, in the cheek, he thought. How I hate him, he thought.

That evening everyone came to his place for dinner – Armand, Odette and Little Marc, and the Alsatians.

His parents had arranged the dining table, the terrace's plastic table, and a small fold-out table borrowed from Armand and Odette, lining them up end to end. His mother had covered them with two identical tablecloths printed with lavender flowers so that the three tables now looked like one long table extending from the dining area onto the terrace. The children would sit at the plastic table at the terrace end.

After his shower, he put on his fluorescent pink shorts and grey T-shirt, on the front of which something was written in the same pink as his shorts, one of the reasons he always wore the two together. He had splashed on a little Signoricci and thought of a few comeback lines should Little Marc comment on it. It was a man's perfume; perfume was for sophisticated people, and so on.

That dinner, with the three tables made into one, that last summer at their holiday house in Cap d'Agde when he was twelve, he sat between Claudia and one of the twins. Little Marc sat on the other side of Claudia. At the adults' end of the table, Armand, being the doyen, sat at the head, with Odette and Claudia's mother beside him.

Halfway through their main course, when it was almost dark outside, Claudia stopped eating. The younger children had abandoned their dinner and were now playing on the terrace. She asked him if he wanted to go for a walk. He nodded, and they left, squeezing between two of the laurel bushes and jumping the terrace's low wall onto the wasteland that one day would be turned into a complex like the *Résidence des Lauriers.* He had fallen many times playing in the wasteland, and his knees still bore the crusted blood from the cuts and scratches he had washed in the shower with stinging soap.

He followed Claudia, a step or two behind, careful where he placed his feet. Claudia walked fast, without hesitation, looking ahead, not down, along the low walls of *Les Lauriers'* houses, their terraces casting faint light onto the wasteland, those without hedges more than those with. At the end of the wasteland she turned left, onto Rue des Pins Marines. Where were they going? On the smooth, lit footpath, he quickened his pace to catch up, staying a little behind and slightly to her left. They hadn't spoken. It looked to him as if she was leading them to the helipad where they had skated.

She was. The tourist office was dark. Only the helipad's northern half was lit, faintly. She crossed the large H in the middle and sat on a bench at the southern end. She looked at him and patted the spot beside her. He sat next to her. He could smell her. How would he describe her scent today? Was it a perfume, a deodorant, her shampoo, soap?

She moved a little closer to him. Her head was turned towards him. He saw her eyes and nose very close. He turned his head away to look around. She placed her right hand on the back of his head. Her left tried to reach a spot on his back, her arm forcing a kind of embrace. He moved his head quickly, gently, left to right and back again, trying to shake off her hand. The hand pushed his head towards hers. Her mouth was on his. He hadn't seen any of it coming. She had seemed not to care for him at all, so why be alone with him now? He closed his eyes. He would open them when the ordeal was over. But when he did open them, he saw her green eyes fixed on him. He had never seen someone's eyes so close, looked into someone's eyes so close that you couldn't see anything in them except what made an eye: the iris and the pupil.

With all this happening, he sat there as if waiting. Then he became aware that something was happening in his pink shorts. It wasn't just their mouths, her tongue. Did she use her tongue to kiss him? At school, among his friends, the tongue, what to do with it when kissing, had become the subject of speculation, stories, theories. You had to move it frantically in circles in the girl's mouth to be a good kisser. No tongue meant no kiss; you hadn't kissed a girl until you had inserted your tongue in her mouth. Did she kiss him with her tongue?

His sex was pushing as if it wanted to escape his shorts. It was hard, trying to stand. It was standing, deforming the fabric at his groin. If only he had worn trousers, or thicker shorts. What to do? This was the most embarrassing thing that had ever happened to him – his sex hard in the presence of a girl. It was more embarrassing than when he had first ejaculated while staying with his aunt in Paris.

He was paralysed. Claudia kept kissing him. He noticed that while kissing him she was trying to roll some of his hair around her right index finger. Where were his arms, his hands?

A booming voice came from the street side of the helipad. He saw Claudia's father approaching with great strides. What had he shouted at them?

Now he said, in a panicked voice, 'Where have you been?' Then something like, 'We've been worried about you!' And then, in an angry voice, 'On your way! Now!'

Claudia got up, said nothing, and followed her father, who was already walking back towards the street.

He remained on the bench, waiting a few moments so his sex could finally rest. It wouldn't. He should follow them, he thought, but he couldn't, not now, not with his sex standing *au garde à vous,* as his father would have said. In his mind, he pictured a sergeant ordering his soldier to rest, and smiled.

Would his father show up as Claudia's had? He

waited a minute or so, and when Claudia and her father were out of sight, he stood up and started for home.

When he got home, everyone had gone. His mother was tidying the tables and his father was smoking a cigar in a chaise longue on the terrace, in the dark. He said nothing to them and went straight to bed.

The following days it was as if he were outside his own life. He spoke little, barely answered his mother when she asked him something. He was elsewhere – where, even today, he can't say. He had the same name, looked the same, perhaps looked a bit different in the mirror, but his life now seemed someone else's. He fell a few times while exploring corners of the wasteland on his own, as he had before, but the scratches didn't sting as much in the evening shower. He could no longer bear his mother coming in to remind him to scrub this or that part of his body, to wash the head of his penis. *N'oublie pas de décaloter!* she still shouted from the kitchen. If only she knew what he was doing with his penis. No, what his penis was doing to him! He now locked the bathroom door before showering.

There was no talk of an apéritif or dinner with Odette and Armand or the Alsatians. He didn't know when he would see Claudia again. The thought of seeing her made him anxious. What would they say to each other? What would they do? Where would she take him this time? What if, by accident, she felt his hard penis? The thought made him frown.

He and his family went to the beach, and he played with the children he had met there, families who always laid their towels and opened their parasols in the same spot, next to his parents' usual place. Their names are gone from his memory now. Their faces too. Only the inflatable canoe one of them owned, brown, with First American-style motifs, remains among his mental images of Cap d'Agde.

It had been a few days without seeing anyone from the residence when he asked his mother when they would have dinner with anyone again. His mother told him that she and his father had decided to sell the house, and that once they had a buyer they would return home. If they couldn't find a buyer by the end of the following week, they would still go home, and his father would come back later to meet the real estate agents and finalise the sale. For now, they were trying to sell the house by posting ads in the local paper. While the end of the next week felt a long way off, the plan seemed sudden. It was not yet mid-August and they would be leaving early. He felt relieved. He started plunging again into the *Langelot* novels at nap time; he looked at Olivia, his old friend, not quite his lover. The fresh memory of Claudia was already changing, becoming a kind of fantastic creature lurking at the edges of thought. The small square window of his mezzanine bedroom was permanently open, and he often thought he heard her voice outside. From the window he could only see the roof of the garage.

One afternoon, after nap time, his mother asked if he could walk up to Armand and Odette's to return a decanter they had left behind after their last dinner together. She washed it again, dried it thoroughly, and sent him on his way, reminding him how fragile it was.

Odette opened the door when he knocked. The dining table inside was already set, layers of plates, silver cutlery, and multiple wine glasses at each place. He noticed places without wine glasses – the children's end of the table. He heard Little Marc's voice asking if it was him at the door. Odette said yes. Marc asked if he could come in; she said yes. He came in and made his way to Little Marc's bedroom, from where the voice had come. As he approached the doorway, he heard a giggle accompanying Marc's voice. He stopped in his tracks. Marc kept talking in his usual rhythm, and the giggle grew louder, until it became a laugh. Marc's head popped out of the bedroom. *Viens!* he said, then disappeared again.

He had never heard Claudia laugh, and he had never seen her lying down. She was laughing now, lying on her side on Marc's bed, watching his show. Marc went to the bed, and Claudia sat up; Marc sat beside her. He stood there at the door, not in the room. Claudia didn't say hello, but looked at him. Did she stop smiling when she saw him? No, she was still caught up in Marc's story. She sat there, tall and long-limbed, back straight, beside chubby, full-cheeked Marc, who had no hair under his nose, not even a faint down. She stood to look at something on a shelf. He looked at her, then at Marc. Now no one spoke. His presence had clearly disturbed whatever had been going on. Claudia had her back turned to them both, and Marc didn't seem to know where to look, while he now stared at Marc. Marc called out, 'Hey, come and sit down,' patting his hands on his lap. Claudia turned and, obeying, went to sit on Marc's lap. She held him by the neck so as not to rock backwards. Marc said she was heavy. He saw no point staying and left. Behind him came variations of Marc's voice and Claudia's giggle.

§

When the holiday house was sold, his father and Jean-Pierre Huré rented a truck and drove down to Cap d'Agde over the Easter long weekend.

Back at school and into other routines at home, he had somehow pushed away the problem of the *Lui* magazine under his mattress. He knew his father would find it. He and Jean-Pierre would lift the mattress and laugh at the discovery. They would instantly understand the role the magazine had played the previous summer. They would be able to read his mind, to enter his most intimate recesses. The thought was daunting, but it didn't haunt him. It lingered there, frightening yet separate from his day-to-day life. He managed to keep it at bay – this was the only solution to the problem of the magazine under the mattress.

He remembers the dinner with Jean-Pierre Huré. His parents had invited him to stay after the long drive from Cap d'Agde. All the furniture of the little house was outside their larger house, packed into the truck his father had rented, now parked on the street. All of it. Everything had fitted in that truck, which hadn't seemed that big. He imagined the beds, as they had been in the house, with their flowery covers and pillows; the dining and outdoor tables, the chairs, the clutter from the garage – what had been in the garage? The red jerrycan his father used to get petrol for the dinghy he had sold that summer; the tools; what else? The chaises longues and the rest of the outdoor furniture, kept there when they weren't at the house… – all piled up in the truck. His father always knew how to pack the car boot; he would have planned the loading in his head and instructed Jean-Pierre where each piece should go, in what order. Some things would not have fitted as imagined, and he would have adjusted his plan on the spot, giving new instructions.

At dinner, his father mentioned the magazine. He said, smiling, looking at him and then at his mother, that they had found *his* magazine, under the mattress. That was how his father referred to it, *his magazine.* There was nothing to say. His young mind quickly began inventing far-fetched explanations to absolve himself of the crimes of owning and hiding a magazine filled with photographs of naked women. But he said nothing. He waited for his father to continue. His father said that the magazine had entertained them during the drive home, that it had kept the boredom of the long drive at bay. This puzzled him. He had never looked at the magazine for more than twenty or thirty minutes at a time. How could it have entertained his father and Jean-Pierre for nine or ten hours in the truck? Jean-Pierre added that some pages had been stuck together and had ripped when separated, and laughed. He didn't remember his magazine having any stuck pages. Perhaps time and the weight of the mattress had caused it. That was all that was said about the magazine.

He never in his adolescence bought another *Lui*. Instead, he collected photographs of women from the mail-order fashion catalogues his mother subscribed to. When she discarded the previous year's catalogue, he would secretly take a few lingerie pages from the pile of old newspapers and magazines by the fireplace. He first hid them under the small cabinet in the upstairs bathroom where he took his baths. But one day his mother moved the cabinet to vacuum underneath, and the pages disappeared. She said nothing. After that, he hid them, folded, inside his *Langelot* novels.

That last summer in Cap d'Agde, his father had packed the car the night before, before his apéritif. In his memory, that early morning had the feeling of late evening; he had a vision of sunset over the pine hills. But they always left Cap d'Agde early in the morning so that, after a late lunch somewhere past the Massif Central, they would be home by seven or eight in the evening. His father was always proud to get them home a little earlier than the year before. They would have a light dinner of charcuterie left from the Cap d'Agde house, with a baguette bought in the village where they'd had lunch. He would feel nostalgic contemplating the deli paper from Cap d'Agde.

But the real sadness, the fresh pain, came when he looked out the back window at the tourist office near the helipad, the church that looked like no other church he'd seen, built recently, not two or three or four hundred years ago, and then, on the left, the pine hills at the bottom of which was their little house among the others of *Les Lauriers.* Each year, the same scene made him shed a few tears. He would whisper, or perhaps just think, some kind of goodbye, some kind of *until next year,* some kind of thank-you to summer, to the holiday house, to the happy times.

Did that last year's departure feel different from those before? The residence was only a few streets from the main road out of Cap d'Agde. Three or four quick turns and the pine hills were behind them, no longer their back garden but the landscape of many past adventures. The scent of the pine trees and the rasp of cicadas' wings would cease to be daily sensations and become memories, the stuff of holidays, for another year. Did he ask himself that morning, looking out the back window, where they would go on holiday the following year? All the departures from Cap d'Agde have become one in his memory, one scene.

The previous evening his father had studied the map with his apéritif and pinpointed a small town a few kilometres off the highway where they would stop for lunch.

He and his father had never had a proper conversation before that day. They had talked about this and that. His father had told him things, had helped him learn irregular English verbs, memorise poems for school. But they had never had a conversation at lunch or dinner where they discussed a topic.

At lunch, in a small town off the highway, north of the Massif Central, about halfway home, with no prelude or warning, his father, who, he sensed, had been watching him more than usual, said, 'You know, you should never try to sleep with a girl too soon.'

Were his parents having coffee and cigarettes while he ate his chocolate mousse? Was the bill on a saucer, covered with the notes to pay it? Were they waiting for the waiter to pick up the money before returning to the car? Had his father planned to say this? Or was he merely filling the silence – the kind that, until they stopped smoking, had always been filled with the smoke of cigars and cigarettes?

His mother exclaimed his father's name.

His father said to her, 'It's true though.'

She shook her head.

To this day he cannot fathom why his father said it. He understood that it must have been connected to Claudia's kiss, and to being found by her father on the bench near the tourist office and helipad. Did Claudia's father think that evening he had tried to *sleep* with Claudia? What did that mean, *to sleep with a girl*? Was the kiss, and his sex stirring in his shorts, already that?

He remembers his mother growing restless, looking out of the restaurant window. Today, looking back, he thinks she seemed to be trying to keep some kind of anger under control. Then, he'd thought she was just impatient to get back on the road.

In the car, returning from weekends at his grandparents' or from holidays, his parents would debrief about the time away, discuss an aunt's laziness in the kitchen, an uncle's political opinions, someone's bossiness, someone else's weight gain since the last visit. No one was spared. And he would listen, amused and privileged. So this is what they think of them; this is what they make of their views, behaviour, appearance… There was something comforting about hearing his parents talk like this in front of him. He listened intently for as long as they went on.

That last summer in Cap d'Agde, he is certain now, there was no such conversation on the trip home. His mother was silent.

At times, his mother would confide in him. Was it often? He remembers one instance in his bedroom at home. She talked about his father not being there – never being there. She said she didn't know where he was or what he was doing. Perhaps he'd been on one of his weekends away with the Cessna co-owners. She started crying and then hugged him. Had she lost her temper with him just before? Was her confession a way to explain herself, to seek forgiveness? It felt as if she wanted him to forgive her for something.

He pretended to pay attention so as not to hurt her feelings. Her tears stirred no sympathy in him, and her stories about his father didn't interest him. In truth, he was always surprised, and perhaps frightened, by his mother's letting her emotions flare up in front of him. He felt trapped. It seemed she was saying to him, Your father is never here, but you are; at least I have you. He tolerated these moments, knowing she would soon compose herself and return to her activities.

No sooner had he become an adult than he went to live on the other side of the world.

In those moments, did she ever mention that last summer in Cap d'Agde? Did she ever talk about the final dinner with their friends from the residence? Why had his parents decided to sell the house? It had seemed abrupt then. Today he wishes he had paid more attention to his mother, to what she said all those years ago. Perhaps today he would not still be asking himself these questions.

An Unequal Love

'I'm happy to send him money for birthdays and Christmas, but what is he going to do with me? He'll be bored with me. What do you want me to say to a twelve-year-old boy?' his aunt had said.

He had no opinion on the matter. 'I don't mind,' he answered when his father asked if he wanted to spend a few days with his aunt in Paris.

'I don't know,' he said when asked if he thought he would be bored with his aunt. Visiting his aunt: he had no opinion on the matter.

Edmonde had just turned thirty-four. She lived alone in her large apartment in the eighth arrondissement of Paris. She didn't work then and read a lot. She had no children.

He saw Paris for the first time leaning forward from the middle of the back seat of the car. His left elbow on his father's seat, his right on his mother's. His mother, too, stared at the view; she didn't come to the capital often. She pointed to a barge on the river where tourists photographed the banks. A *bateau-mouche*, she said, and he was amused by the name.

Later, he was surprised to see, on a pedestal by a bridge and looking out over the Seine, the Statue of Liberty, which he thought was in America. He asked his mother about it. His father said it was a replica, smaller, of the statue in New York.

The Seine was dirty. The Seine had always been dirty, he thought; even in the time of the Gauls it flowed, brown and thick, through Lutetia like a ribbon of mud; never had it been blue like tropical lagoons or clear like bottled water.

The streets of the eighth arrondissement were wide and they, too, were dirty. The grey footpaths were littered with dog excrement; from the car to his aunt's building one had to watch the ground before putting a foot down.

For unclear reasons he expected his aunt to be severe, a woman who didn't smile – a distorted memory of her, perhaps? Something his parents had said? Her reluctance to have him stay? She was all smiles when she opened the door.

'What a handsome boy you are!'

He entered the apartment, where the light was dim, followed by his parents. His father left his small suitcase in the red walled anteroom. They then entered a large room with orange-tapestried walls covered with paintings. It was the lounge and dining room, and daylight would have entered through the long sliding doors if the heavy curtains hadn't been drawn. Beyond the sliding doors, above the garden, ran a long balcony, glimpses of trees appearing when a draught pushed the curtains in or out through the open doors.

Outside light was barred by the thick curtains. Inside, the room was lit by table and floor lamps with low-wattage bulbs.

Along two walls, from floor to ceiling, stood hundreds of books, some yellowed with age, others recent acquisitions.

In front of the books, here and there, stood photographs of relatives in dark wooden frames. He spotted a photo of his parents on their wedding day, his mother in black, her bulging stomach carrying him, a five-month-old foetus, inside.

'The maid is on holidays. It will be just you and me,' Edmonde said. He and his aunt were then about the same height. 'What long feet you have!' she exclaimed.

'He is a size nine,' his mother said. 'Already,' she added after a short silence.

At the mention of his shoe size, he looked up from his feet to the framed drawings above the couch. They were grey. All by the same artist: Michaux, he saw from the careful signature at the bottom right of each, like a pupil's hand. The drawings didn't depict anything – no animals, people, buildings, or objects. They were small monochrome lines and shapes, in Chinese ink. With some imagination, one could perhaps make out human silhouettes in a few.

His mother took his suitcase to a room he had not yet visited. She moved around the apartment as if she lived there. She had now disappeared. His father and his aunt stood talking by the dining table. His father leant against a chair. His mother must have been in the kitchen, for he now heard cups clink, the click-click of the gas ignition, then a pot set on the hob.

The three adults had black tea at the dining table. He sat with them, absent-mindedly listening to talk of family and looking around at the books and artworks. There were sculptures here and there on small tables and pedestals. A life-size bust of a little girl drew him, but he decided to inspect it later.

Then his parents left.

The apartment fell silent. His aunt took the cups and teapot to the kitchen to wash them. He thought he should offer to help with the dishes, but stayed at the table, looking around at the framed pictures and books.

Because his parents had told him she read a lot, he imagined he and his aunt would spend the week on the couch under Michaux's drawings, reading silently and doing nothing else.

'So, what do you want to do?' Edmonde asked, coming out of the kitchen.

§

Back then, his aunt's breasts were higher, rounder. Her face was round, her hair in a bob.

He didn't know what he wanted to do; nor did she know what a twelve-year-old boy might want to do in Paris, or anywhere, outdoors or inside. It was the middle of an autumn afternoon.

He didn't know what he wanted to do, but he knew he didn't want to read. He would rather have played. Either with the miniature Tour de France cyclists he'd left at home, or with a football outside in the street. But in the eighth arrondissement of Paris, he knew, one didn't play with a ball in the street.

She asked whether he wanted to read.

'You know, I have books you might enjoy, with stories for boys your age,' she said.

He shook his head, smiling as he looked around the room.

Then he stood up from the couch where they sat and said, 'I think I'll go for a walk.'

Unsure whether to say yes or no, she said nothing. He walked to the anteroom and, before opening the door, turned to his aunt. She nodded.

Outside, he didn't know where to go. He didn't really want to go out, but he didn't know what to do inside, in his aunt's presence. He left the apartment, crossed the courtyard, passed the garden on his right, and reached the street, the boulevard, rather, turning right. He was careful not to step in dog excrement.

He crossed the wide Avenue de Messine, followed the western arc of the Place de Rio de Janeiro, then walked down Rue de Lisbonne and Rue Monceau until he found himself before a large gilded gate opening onto a park.

In the Parc Monceau – that was the name of the park – he saw ruins of monuments. He crossed paved paths without concern for traffic, since no cars or motorbikes were allowed. He walked, looking up at the tops of the tall trees. At one point he saw marble busts that held no interest for him. He walked on the soft, thick lawn. He stopped for a good half hour at a merry-go-round with life-size wooden horses. He watched its patrons; some laughed and neighed like horses. They were adults. He smiled to himself at the salacious jokes loudly made by a middle-aged man on one of the horses.

Then he found his way back to his aunt's building, retracing his steps.

When he returned from his walk – an hour and a half long – Edmonde was bent over a small notebook at the card table in the corner of the living room. She held a ballpoint pen; a couple of pencils lay nearby;

she gave the impression she was doing her homework.

She stopped writing and closed the notebook when he came in. 'I'm going to unpack,' he said, and went to his room. She smiled up at him from where she sat.

In the evening, after he had spent some time on his bed day-dreaming and dozing, he went to the main room, where Edmonde was still writing in her notebook.

'Are you hungry?' she asked.

He nodded, and she left her small table, disappearing into the kitchen.

The dining-room table was set; she must have done it while he was out walking or in his room. Between the two plates and their cutlery stood two wine glasses and a half-consumed bottle of red, the cork protruding a centimetre or two above the neck.

From the kitchen, Edmonde brought a plate of

thin pink-orange slices and a small basket of bread wrapped in a white serviette. He smelt the warmth of the toasted brown slices.

'Perhaps you'd prefer white wine,' his aunt said.

'No. Water, please.'

'Don't you drink wine at home?'

'At family gatherings. With water.'

'Your father mixes your wine with water?' she asked, surprised.

'Mum.'

'I see. And your father says nothing when your mother pours water into your wine?'

'No.'

Dinner consisted of smoked salmon slices, a few lettuce leaves, and cheese. There was also a cake from the pâtisserie downstairs. He didn't drink any wine, out of timidity. He almost changed his mind when he saw his aunt lick her lips after each sip. He didn't take a second slice of chocolate cake, also out of timidity. By the end of dinner the bottle was empty. He was still hungry.

'Have you had enough to eat?' she asked.

'Yes, yes.'

'Why don't you have a shower before bed? I'll clear the table.'

Naked in the large bathroom, illuminated by ceiling lights and, above the sink, a square of bulbs around the mirror like an actor's dressing-room, he didn't know what to do with his clothes. He didn't want Edmonde to find them, as they were dirty, especially his underpants, which were often stained with a brown mark. He rolled them up and decided to hide them in his suitcase.

He massaged his scalp vigorously so the shampoo would spread evenly through his hair, down to the roots. Foam ran down his face and into his ears. He closed his eyes. He heard something, a small noise, in the bathroom. He rinsed his hair, holding his breath. He wiped his eyes and opened the shower curtain. Edmonde was there, sitting on the toilet.

She smiled at him. He retreated into the shower, closed the curtain, and stood still. Through the rush of the shower he heard the toilet flush, then water run in the basin, then nothing. He slowly opened the curtain. Edmonde was gone. Quickly he scrubbed himself with the soapy bath glove, rinsed, and stepped out of the shower.

As he dried himself, he saw that the rolled-up clothes, with his underpants inside, were gone.

§

The next morning, at breakfast at the dining table, neither he nor Edmonde spoke. When he'd come into the main room, Edmonde asked if he'd slept well, and he said yes. While they ate toast with blood-orange and forest-berry jam and drank black tea, she read a thick book, and he looked around the room. Day or night, morning or afternoon, the curtains were always drawn and the same lamps lit the room.

After breakfast he brushed his teeth, dressed, made his bed, and closed his bedroom window as rain began to fall. His mother had packed his school exercise books, and he saw no alternative but to take them to the main room, sit at the table, and complete his French or maths exercises.

Edmonde sat on the couch in the same sky-blue silk dressing gown she'd worn at breakfast, reading the same book and smoking a cigarette. Her legs were folded to her left side; her toes wriggled now and then.

He asked for a pencil and an eraser. 'Look on the table,' she said, pointing to the card table with her two notebooks. 'I don't own an eraser, though.' At the dining table, on the white tablecloth marked with a few wine stains, he opened his French exercise book.

He had noticed that his aunt smoked a lot. Sitting in the same room for hours, it seemed to him she smoked continuously. He now realised that the faint haze and the sweet, acrid scent floating in the apartment came from his aunt's cigarettes.

When he had first entered the apartment the previous afternoon, and later returned from the Parc Monceau, the pale smoke had enveloped him like an esoteric vapour. Edmonde's cigarettes had an unusual scent, and when smoked, they left an aroma closer to burnt jasmine incense than tobacco. The smoke neither filled the apartment completely nor vanished through the perpetually open sliding doors.

And so, in that strange ether, they spent the morning.

Edmonde had made triangle-shaped sandwiches with the smoked salmon left over from the night before. It was their lunch. He had to make a tremendous effort to swallow the dill sauce and capers in the sandwiches. At one point he thought he might vomit, but he did his best not to show his disgust. Edmonde mostly gazed absently outside, through the sliding doors whose curtains were slightly open. At one point he thought she might be watching the swallows' comings and goings, but her gaze, he realised, had no real focus.

After lunch he was still hungry, and the taste of dill and capers lingered in his mouth. No matter how much water he drank or saliva he swallowed, the taste persisted.

As he and Edmonde took the plates and glasses to the kitchen, he began to wonder what they would do that afternoon. He couldn't spend the afternoon on his exercise books! And he didn't fancy a walk in the Parc Monceau in the rain. And now that she'd finished her small cup of coffee and the dining table was clear, save for a few breadcrumbs on the lace cloth, with the plates, cutlery and glasses piled in the sink, Edmonde glanced around the kitchen and said, 'Why don't I take you to the Orangerie?'

The Orangerie. Orange trees. He reluctantly smiled and acquiesced.

They put on their jackets and left the apartment. The rain had stopped. Edmonde carried her small white leather purse in her right hand and held his right hand with her left. Holding his aunt's hand gave him a strange sensation. Her hand was soft, and she held his loosely, not in the tight grip he was used to from his mother. His mother used to hold his hand to stop him running off or to keep him at her pace, though she hadn't held his hand for some time now, since he wasn't little anymore. He wasn't sure why his aunt held his hand. They walked slowly to the nearby métro station without saying much.

The Orangerie, it occurred to him as they queued at the entrance of a large building resembling a temple, was a museum, not an orange orchard. Above the monumental doorway was a pediment carved with plants.

At the counter, a sign read: twenty francs for adults, ten for children.

He told Edmonde he had been to museums before, with his school. The year before, he had visited the Archaeological Museum of Saint-Germain-en-Laye, where he saw the enormous antler of a prehistoric stag. And a few weeks earlier, his French teacher had taken the class to Émile Zola's house in Médan.

His aunt, in her light and friendly voice, said she didn't see the point of visiting a dead writer's house. He told her the house was very close to the train tracks, which seemed to make her think.

At the Saint-Germain-en-Laye museum, he'd run from one display to another, spending only a few seconds on exhibits that didn't interest him. He and his classmates had been free to wander the museum at their leisure. When he spotted the antler high on the wall at the far end of the long room, he ran to it. As he approached, he could hardly believe how large it was. He stood beneath the stag's antler for a long while, trying to fathom how huge the beast that had carried it must have been. That night, in his dreams, he saw the giant prehistoric stag in the forest and heard its powerful bellow. The beast was ten times taller and larger than the stags he'd seen in the forests around his home in Normandy. Its features weren't as fine as those of modern stags; the extinct beast looked cruel and demonic, but in the dream he had kept his distance, hiding from it.

Walking slowly at his aunt's pace on the carpeted floor of the Orangerie, spending several minutes before each picture, was rather tedious. There were no other children in the museum, and that concerned him. Perhaps he shouldn't have been there. And why was a child's ticket cheaper than an adult's? He looked half-heartedly at the paintings while Edmonde remained silent, smiling faintly, seemingly at the artworks.

At one point, looking at a painting by Soutine called *The Choirboy*, she said the boy reminded her of him.

The boy was very ugly. Why did the ugly boy in the picture remind her of him? Hadn't she said he was handsome? How could a scrawny, ugly boy remind someone of a handsome one?

As if guessing his puzzlement, she said that, first, he seemed as well-behaved as a choirboy, and then, correcting herself, that choirboys were merely the best-behaved of boys. Second, the choirboy in the picture was about his age, slim and dark-haired like him. Third, she could see on his face, as on the boy's, the turmoil of adolescence brewing.

He said nothing in return. What did she mean by 'the turmoil of adolescence'? The remark concerned him instantly.

'I'm not an adolescent,' he snapped.

'Aren't you?'

A little later, she asked what he thought of Soutine's paintings. He said he didn't know.

But he thought Soutine didn't draw well, that his colours were darkened – even his whites – and often smudged. Yet somehow his paintings, with Douanier Rousseau's, were his favourites so far. At school, his own paintings were often smudged, and the art teacher had told him off: Make an effort not to smudge your colours! But that had seemed impossible to him.

Soutine had painted a carcass! *Side of Beef*, the painting was called. 'Why would anyone want to paint a bloody carcass?' he asked Edmonde. She asked if he wanted to hear the story behind it. He said yes.

'Soutine had a great admiration for Rembrandt. In homage to Rembrandt's *The Carcass of an Ox*, which is at the Louvre (I'll take you there one day), he set out to paint a cow's carcass. So he bought a carcass from the butcher and hung it in his studio. It took him several days to finish the painting, and each day he sent his model, a young girl he'd painted before, to the butcher to fetch blood and flesh to somehow refurbish the stinking carcass. The neighbours were disgusted by the stench, the swarm of flies that had invaded the building, and perhaps by the very idea of flesh left to rot in a studio for no reason.'

The story made him smile.

Why would Soutine, or Rembrandt, paint a carcass? he wondered.

In Soutine's paintings he saw what he would later call torment; in Rousseau's, joy. In both, and in many other painters at the museum, he saw a kind of childishness. He thought of the painters shown at the Orangerie as people with a child's mind: what they painted was either childish in subject – a doll, Pierrot and Harlequin, a child playing with figurines – or childish in manner, with naïve figures and smudged colours.

Matisse painted naked women, but most were large and neither well drawn nor well painted. He had once drawn a portrait of his maternal grandfather, and thought it much better than Matisse's drawings of naked women.

Was painting naked women pleasurable? Uncomfortable?

Though as clumsily painted as Matisse's, he found Modigliani's nudes painted after 1915 more appealing. He thought it might be the colour of their skin, glowing with an orange patina, and the rounded shape of their bodies.

Edmonde pointed to a painting of Louis Berlioz's house on the opposite wall, and they walked over to it. She said she often listened to Berlioz at home and had been to many concerts of his music. The humility of Berlioz's house in Montmartre had always surprised her. Every time she came to the Orangerie, the painting had the same effect: What a humble house, she would say to herself. From what the painting showed – the two façades at the corner of Rue Saint-Denis and Rue Saint-Vincent – it seemed the house had barely any windows, or even an entrance.

'Utrillo,' Edmonde said 'only ever painted one

neighbourhood of Paris: Montmartre. He painted, again and again, a small part of a street or a corner, or a building, like Berlioz's house or the *mairie* with its flags. All his life he painted Montmartre.

'He lived with his mother and was a drunk… By your age, already a drunk… He certainly didn't mix his wine with water or drink only at family gatherings… He had no family, apart from his mother, who was also a painter, and he drank himself drunk every day.

'On reflection, I probably shouldn't encourage you to drink wine without water. We wouldn't want to send you back to your parents drunk like Utrillo, or with a taste for a bottle or two a day.'

Before leaving the museum, Edmonde took him to the souvenir shop and bought him postcards of some of the paintings they'd seen. Among them were Douanier Rousseau's *Child with Doll* and Soutine's *Choirboy*.

They hadn't planned to go for a walk in the park, but here they were, strolling through the Jardin des Tuileries. She held his right hand in her left and her handbag in her right. He carried the postcards in a small, thin brown paper bag in his left hand.

§

When they got home, Edmonde put on a record of Berlioz. *Harold en Italie.*

That evening, while listening to Berlioz, they ate the *blanquette de veau* they'd bought at the local delicatessen on their way back from the Orangerie. She had a glass of Burgundy. Halfway through the blanquette, she offered him a sip from her glass, which he accepted.

The wine, without water, tasted sour to him. She saw it on his face and, smiling, said that while he was in her house, his wine wouldn't be mixed with water.

'You ought to start liking wine, without water. No one in the family dislikes wine…' She went on to say that perhaps he was too young to appreciate wine, that it would come later in life.

They each ate an *opéra* for dessert, she with a glass of port.

After dinner, Edmonde cleared the table and did the dishes while he went to the bathroom for his shower.

He was in the shower. It would be a quick one – today he wasn't washing his hair. In fact, he had decided not to wash his hair again until he returned home, to shorten his showers and lessen the chance of Edmonde needing the toilet while he was naked.

Then, as on the previous day, a noise. He turned off the water and pulled the shower curtain open a little, hiding his body behind it. Edmonde was sitting on the toilet. This time, the toilet lid was closed, and her underwear wasn't down at her feet. She was sitting, it seemed to him, like a spectator.

She smiled at him. 'You're handsome,' she said.

She asked him something. He wasn't sure what she meant, though he recognised the question's central word from school. He wasn't sure exactly what it meant. His aunt wasn't giggling like the girls at school who'd once asked one of his friends the same question.

'What?' he said.

'Do you wank?' she said. 'Masturbating means wanking. I used the verb in its reflexive form. Later in life, you might use it transitively.'

He didn't think he did such a thing. Could one masturbate without knowing?

'I don't think so,' he said, careful to keep himself hidden behind the shower curtain.

She smiled and told him he'd know if he did, so to her, his answer was no. 'Okay,' he said.

She suggested he look it up in the dictionary sometime.

'Yes,' he said.

He decided to close the shower curtain and resume washing. He thought he heard the door open and close; he pulled the curtain back to check, and she was gone. He quickly scrubbed himself with the soapy bath glove, rinsed off, and stepped out of the shower.

§

The first time he walked in the Parc Monceau, he walked briskly. He had paid little attention to what was there, except for the merry-go-round.

The second time, he walked slowly, taking his time, looking here and there. He sought a corner, a small place where he could hide and be alone. These past days at his aunt's apartment, he had been denied his privacy. In his bedroom and in the bathroom, he couldn't lock the doors; he was constantly on his guard. At any moment, his solitude could be broken. This precarious solitude, he felt, wasn't solitude at all, for when solitude was precarious, he was never truly free. He was always expecting his aunt's intrusion and couldn't concentrate on anything.

He imagined there might be a spot in the park, under a tree, where no one would see or find him, where he could be alone and regain his sense of privacy.

With his hands in his trouser pockets and his jacket hood up, though it wasn't raining or cold, he inspected clusters of trees and isolated parterres.

He sat on the grass behind some shrubs, hidden from sight. He could barely hear a voice, only the faint hum of distant traffic; children's cries and the murmur of voices. He was filled with an incomprehensible embarrassment. It dawned on him that his aunt now seemed always to be on his mind when he wasn't with her. Here he was, sitting alone, hidden, free to think about his school friends, about his *chérie*, Sophie Rédolfi, and in his mind, he saw his aunt. For some reason, his imagination summoned his aunt. And she was shirtless before him; though her brassiere mercifully covered her breasts, he knew they were there, round and plump. She turned her back to him, yet her head turned slightly toward him, and she smiled. At him. Her legs, slightly parted, and her behind seemed angled toward him, as if she wanted him to look. Later, she lay like one of Matisse's women, on her side, on the couch, her silk gown half open, and she looked at him as he sat at the table, pondering a maths problem in his exercise book. He didn't see her pubis or breasts, but he saw her stomach and her bare left leg, and could naturally imagine where the rest was. In fact, his gaze now lingered more insistently on the place where he knew her pubis was.

On the grass, in that secluded corner, he didn't know what to do with these images, which elicited new feelings, both embarrassing and exhilarating at once.

§

Although she was old, he found his aunt beautiful. More beautiful than his mother. And more than his French and English teachers. He knew she was old, yet he saw something young in her. A childlike smile, a youthful hairstyle, and the way she looked at people.

One morning after breakfast, after tidying his room, while she read on the couch in her usual position, smoking, he decided to talk to her rather than do his maths exercises. He told her again that he had visited Émile Zola's house a few weeks earlier.

She put her book down and waited for him to go on. He didn't; all he'd wanted was to say he had visited Zola's house, and now he waited for her to respond. He had noticed the many Zola volumes in her Pléiade collection.

'You're too young to read Zola, so I'm baffled as to why your teacher took you to his house,' Edmonde said. 'Are you reading Zola at school?'

'No.'

'Good.'

'At the moment we're reading *The Invisible Man* by Herbert George Wells. We'll soon have to complete a *fiche de lecture*, but I've already finished it. I've also read *Five Little Pigs* by Agatha Christie, even though it wasn't for school.'

She talked about Hercule Poirot and how comical a character he was. He said Poirot was very clever.

'Yes, he is,' she said, and wondered how Hercule Poirot's English would be rendered in French. Poirot's English was often structured like French, which was why she always enjoyed reading the stories in English – for the way he spoke, which made her smile, and for the plots, of course

'Don't read Zola,' she said. 'Read him later. When you're older. When you're old. Same with Proust: wait until you've lived a little, until you've seen more of the world than family and school. Don't read them at school. You don't read at school, you follow a programme. Read Agatha Christie, read Wells, read Wilde's tales, read Jack London, Swift, Stevenson, Mark Twain. You need to know Huck Finn, White Fang, Hawk-eye and the Mohicans. Then spend time with Tartarin de Tarascon and Poil de Carotte. Read Frédéric Mistral, and Maupassant's stories after that. I could tell you what reading does to you, where it takes you, but perhaps you won't like it and you won't read. I'm not your teacher, your father, or your mother. All I'll say is that people in books, in stories, make far better company than your teachers, your parents, or me. Often you find that the stories are about you.'

This left him thoughtful: How could a story be about me when the author doesn't know I exist? How could a dead writer write about me before I was even born? Most writers are dead.

Edmonde had gone back to her book, and he told her that a few weeks earlier he'd scored a good mark in *rédaction*. She looked up at him, taking her reading glasses off.

'I wrote it at home,' he said.

'What was the subject?' she asked.

It was a little different from the usual 'In five pages, relate your last holidays.' On that occasion, they had to describe a pedantic person.

(Although the mark was good, it wasn't the highest, as he'd expected. Over the weekend he had asked his mother, then his father, what 'pedantic' meant. His mother's answer was closer to the dictionary's than his father's. But he couldn't think of anyone particularly pedantic. He thought of his father, whom he now saw as rather pedantic, now that he understood the word. His father was tall, slim, well-dressed, smoked cigars, and always half-listened to others, which, to his mind, gave him a pedantic air, but his father was also funny and tender, and not so good at maths or French, and he thought to be pedantic one had to speak polished French. His father didn't. He had thought briefly of his aunt but couldn't recall her well enough to find pedantic traits. He thought of his dead grandfather but could remember only his aquiline nose and the hair sprouting from his ears and nostrils. Two physical traits weren't enough to paint a pedantic portrait.

Lacking a suitable candidate, he made a list of

qualities his pedantic person should have. Well-dressed; aquiline nose; spoke unusually polished French; looked at others haughtily, etc.

Then one person came to mind, because of the aquiline nose. That person had an aquiline nose, he was sure of it, and all the other traits seemed to fit too. He didn't smoke cigars but cigarettes – in a cigarette holder… He opened *Five Little Pigs* and flicked through until he found it. Yes, there it was! A detailed description of Hercule Poirot. Copied in his handwriting, it filled just under four pages. So he added a few descriptive paragraphs, which he didn't like. They seemed clumsy beside Agatha Christie's, and even contradicted her (Poirot wasn't tall; he was short). So he copied it again, this time broadening his letters so the text filled nearly five pages.

He had expected the highest mark – after all, Agatha Christie was a famous author, and surely she deserved it.

He thought perhaps the teacher didn't like his handwriting. Perhaps she just wasn't a good teacher. In any case, since he hadn't got the top mark, he wasn't the best at rédaction in the class, and that had bothered him.)

'Who did you describe?' Edmonde asked.

He smiled and went through the list of traits he had chosen to describe someone pedantic, changing the cigars to cigarettes in a holder.

She smiled, said it was very good, and picked up her book again.

§

She asked whether he'd like to come with her to the pâtissier downstairs. He said he was happy to stay in the apartment, perhaps he could set the dinner table. She smiled, said it was a good idea, and left.

He set the table with two wine glasses, and she still

wasn't back. He went into her bedroom. The bed was unmade, and clothes – her white trousers, blouses, socks, beige bras and panties – were draped over a chair and the bed's brass footboard. Her wardrobe was open; mostly white clothes hung inside in a loose disorder.

The bottom sheet of her bed was creased. The curtains were drawn. Did she ever open them? The sliding doors to the balcony were open. On her two bedside tables and the commode, she had divided the flowers she had bought the day before into vases. On the wall near the wardrobe were black-and-white photographs pinned up. Photos of people he didn't know, and one of François, whom he remembered from early childhood. Then he noticed a photo of a younger Edmonde with a beautiful woman. His aunt was beautiful in the photo, but the other woman, her arm around Edmonde's shoulder, was the most beautiful woman he'd ever seen. She had shoulder-length black hair, a fringe, and large dark eyes that seemed to smile.

He ran out of the bedroom. Sat on the couch. She still wasn't back. How long could it take to buy a cake, downstairs? He looked around. His gaze settled on the card table, with its pens, pencils, and two closed notebooks on the green felt surface. He got up and went to the table.

The handwriting in the first notebook was fine and small. The capital letters weren't formed the way he'd been taught at school. Most were shaped like printed capitals. Some of the lowercase letters too, particularly the 'r' and 'f', he noticed. The first notebook was filled with this handwriting, front to back, every page covered from top to bottom. How could anyone have written so much? he wondered.

Her name appeared several times on each page; he also saw her late husband's name – 'François' – and the name 'Lucia'.

He still hadn't heard his aunt open the front door, take off her coat, and hang it on the rack in the anteroom. She still hadn't come back. He opened the second notebook. He opened it from the back.

The second notebook wasn't finished. About a third of the pages were filled with his aunt's writing. He felt less overwhelmed by the busyness of the pages and read the last page and a half Edmonde had written.

> *. . . We walked up the mountain. It was a spring afternoon; we heard cuckoos in the trees, and the soft rays of the sun wrapped us in gentle warmth. Soon I began to sweat. Edmonde and François were sweating too; they had started before me. Edmonde was dressed in white trousers and a white blouse, which I'd told her would get dirty on the walk. She didn't care, she said she expected them to. 'One doesn't wear white*

to keep one's clothes clean,' she declared. The sweat rings under her arms widened as we walked, while François's back was drenched.

I began to sweat and to smell; I could smell my vagina beneath my dress, sweating out François's seed that had stayed with me after I'd showered. I was embarrassed. I thought, I'll wash myself in the river when we get there. The three of us could swim in the river and wash off the sweat. So I thought of the river. I remembered it well; it was only a couple of hours' walk from the village where I'd grown up. I'd swum in that river as a little girl…

Did he hear something? He closed the notebook, went back to the couch, and waited for his aunt to return. He couldn't make sense of what he had read.

Three grown-ups walking up a mountain to swim in a river near a village, but he sensed there was more to it. He too had swum naked in rivers with friends. Three adults swimming in a river made him think of the adults riding the wooden horses on the merry-go-round – they seemed out of place.

The word 'vagina', reading it in his aunt's notebook, made him uneasy.

Not long after he'd closed the second notebook, she came home smiling, carrying two boxes from a different pâtisserie. 'I thought I'd walk to Lenôtre,' she said. He saw the words 'Lenôtre' on the boxes.

§

One morning, the morning after, as it happened, she took him into her bedroom and showed him the paintings on the wall. Beside her bed hung an austere *nature morte* of rotting apples on a table, which to him looked almost photographic, the apples and table rendered with such precision and vitality. Facing the bed was a large, naïve, orange painting of a cemetery in Chile, which she had bought when François took her there. She said she had bought it with a friend of François's named Lucia.

'When we lived in Chile, Lucia and I decided to share it. She'd have it for a year, then I would, and so on. When François died and I was about to return to France, she gave it to me. She said she thought I should have it.'

Then Edmonde fell silent, perhaps to let him admire the painting, or perhaps because she'd been taken back to Chile, to the company of François and Lucia.

'She decided to give it to me for good, after François died.'

Another silence.

'She was François's lover.'

Silence.

'She was our lover. She was beautiful.'

She walked to the wall of photographs and pointed to the one he had seen the day before, to the beautiful woman with shoulder-length dark hair, a fringe, and large black eyes.

'That's Lucia,' she said, looking at him with a small smile. Then, as if she had read his thoughts the day before, she looked again at the picture and asked, 'Isn't she the most beautiful of women? The most beautiful woman you've ever seen?'

He did not respond; he stared at the photograph.

That night in bed, the faces of his aunt and Lucia appeared to him. Pressed together. They were kissing. He opened his eyes. In the living room there was a wall of art books, and he knew some of them contained paintings of naked women. He went to the living room. The floor lamp by the art-book shelves was still lit, like all the others. He opened a book on Modigliani and flipped through it. No reclining nude with folded arms behind her head; no nude looking over her right shoulder. Then he opened a book on Paul Signac. A picture showed a woman at her toilette, arms raised to fix a pin in her hair, but she was wearing a heavy purple corset. Each book he opened felt heavy on his lap. He looked for Matisse but couldn't find him. He hadn't found a naked woman; he hadn't even known where to look. His aunt might have got up, hearing the rustle of pages in the living room, and asked what he was looking for in those books. He rose from the couch, looked down the short corridor to his aunt's bedroom, and saw light under the door. He guessed she was reading. He went back to bed, and his aunt's and Lucia's faces were still pressed together. Their naked bodies too, standing before him as if calling him, and he kept his eyes closed. After a while, Lucia disappeared, and only his aunt remained before him. She turned away but kept her gaze on him, smiling. Her bottom faced him, the upper part of her body slightly turned towards him. Her long, slender arms. He saw her right breast, its nipple, and she looked him in the eyes with her eternal smile.

When they met at breakfast, he thought she knew. It must be on my face, on my trousers, he thought. He had hidden his pyjama bottoms in the zippered compartment of his suitcase, but the smell seemed to linger, to still be there. It couldn't be, he told himself, and he tried to reassure himself that the smell, which somehow reminded him of the chlorinated water at the local swimming pool, was only in his nostrils. But she had guessed, he was certain of it, it must be on my hand, he said to himself.

He said nothing at breakfast. Nor did she. She didn't ask if he'd slept well. She posed no questions.

She must know, he thought, otherwise she would speak to me. But then, she had rarely spoken to him over breakfast – not the day before, or the day before that, before it happened. Still, all he could think was that she knew, and that she felt sorry for him, ashamed for him.

All day he thought about it, or so he thinks he remembers. All those years ago. What did he and Edmonde do that day? He can't remember. Did they go out? Did he sit at the table to do his French or maths exercises? She had known nothing of his inner turmoil. How could she? There was nothing on his hand; she couldn't see the pyjama bottoms he'd already taken off to put on his corduroy trousers, over which he had decided to keep his dressing gown. They most likely had an ordinary day.

He remembers that in the evening, Edmonde had told him that next time she would take him to the Louvre. They could easily spend two or three days exploring it. The Louvre also had a wonderful souvenir shop, where one could buy resin replicas of sculptures and prints of paintings. And, of course, postcards. He had decided to start collecting postcards from museums. *Choirboy* and *Child with Doll* were the first two. He had written almost the same short account of their visit to the Orangerie on the back of the other postcards he had bought there, and sent them to his parents and grandparents.

That last evening together, he remembers it clearly now, they had an apéritif. She gave him a little port in a small tulip glass. She had made canapés of smoked salmon. There were no capers on the canapés. They had sat on the couch, and after a sip or two of port, he had smiled, looking around. He had felt the warmth of the port spreading through him, and he had looked at his aunt and told her she was beautiful. He told her he liked her smile, her voice, and her hair. He told her he had found Lucia very beautiful, and that perhaps one day he too would have a lover as beautiful as she was. She had smiled and moved to him, taking his face in both hands and giving him a quick, smacking kiss on the lips.

There wasn't going to be any dinner. She hadn't set the dinner table. On the couch, after the smoked salmon canapés, they ate macaroons and éclairs from Lenôtre while drinking port.

Later that evening – he had forgotten it was that day – his parents picked him up.

His mother was annoyed that Edmonde had given him alcohol and that he hadn't packed his suitcase; she packed it for him.

It was late when they left. In the car, he soon began to doze. He tried to keep his eyes open to see the lights of Paris, but on the *périphérique* and through its tunnels he saw little of the city. In the night, the yellow lights of the cars on one side of the road irritated his eyes. He looked ahead at the red lights of the cars in front; their energy and intensity were different, deeper, more inward, than the yellow lights. The red lights called for his attention, urged him to follow their movement, to be aware of the danger in their motion. That was their force. The yellow headlights showed the road, its lines and borders, and they hurt his eyes. His father, like him, kept his eyes on the road. He decided to keep fighting his sleepiness. His mother was already asleep, her mouth a little open. His father alone would be awake if he'd fallen asleep.

www.ingramcontent.com/pod-product-compliance
Lightning Source LLC
LaVergne TN
LVHW041103080826
845145LV00007B/1670

* 9 7 8 1 7 6 3 6 0 0 9 5 9 *